FROM THE WORLD OF VERDA

LEVIATHAN

AN ASHER & AVANDRIELL STORY

PHILIP C. QUAINTRELL

For Those who need a little more Asher in their life...

ALSO BY PHILIP C. QUAINTRELL

DRAMATIS PERSONAE

Adilandra Draqaro
Princess of Illian

Aenwyn Kirion
Elven Ambassador

Asher
Ranger

Athis Draqaro
Prince of Illian

Avandriell
Bronze dragon, bonded with Asher

Balthazar Blackhelm
Pirate Lord

Doran Heavybelly
King of Dhenaheim

Galanör Reveeri
Elven Ambassador

Gideon Thorn
Dragon Rider

Gwenyfer Valayan
Queen of Erador

Hadarax
Giant

Ilargo
Green dragon, bonded with Gideon

Inara Draqaro
Queen of Illian/Commander of the Guardians of the Realm

Kassian Kantaris
Master of the mage school, Ikirith

Vighon Draqaro
King of Illian

THE STORY SO FAR...

A Clash of Fates brought an end to The Fated War, scattering Verda's heroes to futures they fought and bled for.

Illian and all within its borders are ruled by Vighon and Inara Draqaro, the House of the Flaming Sword. Their children are Athis, so named for Inara's dragon, and Adilandra, so named for her grandmother. For seventeen years, they fostered Gwenyfer Valayan, the rightful queen of Erador, who now sits upon that western throne.

Gideon Thorn and his dragon, Ilargo, worked tirelessly for years to secure peace in Erador, thereby allowing Gwenyfer to rule without threat of death. Their task complete, the pair now roam the world in search of potential Riders, who might awaken the dormant eggs in Drakanan.

Galanör and Aenwyn, who pledged themselves to Queen Reyna and King Nathaniel of Ayda, were gifted the station of ambassadors. They call Illian their home and work always to aid the world of man on behalf of the elven nation.

The icy realm of Dhenaheim was left in the grips of monsters,

1

who invaded upon the dwarven halls in their absence. King Doran, son of Dorain, sought to uproot the fiends and make safe his peoples' home once more. He did this after several years of hardship and yet more fighting, and with the help of an old friend and his young dragon.

Asher and Avandriell gave years to the dwarves, hunting monsters in the dark places of the world. It was their great pleasure to do so, enjoying their time amongst Doran's kin. In the years since, leading to Queen Gwenyfer's departure from Illian astride Ilargo, life had never been so sweet for the ranger and his intrepid dragon—and well earned it was.

1

THE HUNT

The snow crunched under his boots, the powder all too fresh, even in a village so sleepy as Hogstead. There should have been evidence of a hundred people living their lives, their prints muddying the streets up and down. The region hadn't known snow for two days. That was two days in which the village must have lay dormant, desolate, *dead*.

The latter had brought a ranger into its midst.

Asher crouched down, his green cloak fanning across the ground behind him. With one hand, he bore down through the snow and wiped it away.

Blood.

Splattered across the hard ground, it had frozen, a dark secret beneath nature's purest blanket.

The ranger sighed, his hot breath spoiling the air. He had never wanted a contract to be so wrong, imagining the lack of contact with Longdale, the village's lifeline to real civilisation, was due to the particularly harsh winter.

"They've probably been bedding down for a few weeks," the ranger had said, his words aimed at the very lord of Longdale, from whom the contract had found patronage.

"Gods be damned," he cursed, tossing his handful of snow away.

Rising to his full height, it was with patient and experienced eyes that he surveyed all that he could of Hogstead. From the road, if it could be given so grand a name, he could only see half a dozen buildings, and they were all coated in thick snow. Still, Asher noted the damage here and there.

A broken window frame.

Discarded supplies poking through the snow.

A door hanging from a single hinge.

A house with no door at all, its threshold piled with intruding snow.

Then there was the lack of smoke. Not a single chimney revealed the fire that should have been battling the bitter cold, keeping the inhabitants of Hogstead warm. It seemed the shadows were Hogstead's only inhabitants, not to be beaten back by even a mere candle.

The village had no more life than the rocky hills that surrounded it.

A well-developed sixth sense informed Asher that a fight was in his imminent future.

As he would, the ranger made a check of his weaponry. The hilt on his hip was as familiar as it was reassuring, the grip a tight binding of dark green leather to match his cloak. His fingers moved up to the pommel, where he could press his thumb into the blunt studs that decorated the sphere.

Feeling he would need it in a hurry, the ranger pulled on the sword, drawing it no more than a couple of inches to ensure the blade hadn't frozen in the scabbard. He glimpsed those inches, sighting what looked like dull steel under the grey clouds. Knowing it was not steel made Asher feel two-feet taller.

He still recalled the moment Doran Heavybelly had presented it to him, deep in the halls of the newly-reclaimed Grimwhal, the dwarf's home city.

"Ye've more than earned it," the king of Dhenaheim had said to him, the weapon held horizontally in the hands of the smith beside him.

Asher knew well the part he had played in liberating the dark tunnels of the dwarven realm, though he doubted it had been enough to see any dwarf part with so fine a blade. He also knew of the dwarven tradition where weapons were concerned. Being the one who intended to wield it, he had taken the sword from the one who had forged it, concluding his ownership and, in the eyes of the dwarves, the sword's loyalty.

With thirty-five inches of tempered *silvyr*, the double-edged sword was an arsenal unto itself. It was also worth a fortune for those who cared about such things.

Running his hand across his belt, he felt the two throwing knives before going on to find the curved dagger near the base of his back. With his other hand, the ranger tugged on the straps that cut across his chest, securing the quiver across his shoulders. It was laden with arrows, each destined to find its end in some monster.

By the weight of it, Asher knew his folded bow was hooked to the quiver—his oldest... anything. Not that it retained any of its original parts, the bow worked and reworked so many times since his days in the service of Nightfall.

Rounding out his mobile armoury, the ranger reached over his shoulder and gripped the hilt of his short-sword. As he had with the two-handed broadsword, he removed the blade a few inches to make certain it hadn't frozen in place. Like its larger sibling, the weapon boasted an hourglass blade of pure silvyr. While its shape and size were remnants of his life as an assassin, the weapon itself had been forged by a dwarven smith with the purest of hearts.

He would look in on Danagarr soon, he promised himself.

First things first...

The crunching snow announced his every step. For the second time in his life, Asher entered the village of Hogstead in search of a monster. He wasn't dealing with a Giant this time—their obtuse handiwork was always clear to see. This was something else, something that possessed a touch of real evil in its heart.

Coming across the house with no door, the ranger paused over the threshold and peered inside, one hand resting on the hilt of his broadsword. Asher narrowed his eyes, piercing the gloom therein. A family had lived inside, their belongings, including small wooden toys, were strewn about, scattered amongst the debris and broken furniture.

More blood.

It was splattered up the walls and interior door frames. Dark red hand prints could be seen inside the small kitchen. It was the blood on the floor that caught Asher's eye, where it could be seen in thick lines. The red smears suggested that more than one body had been dragged from the rooms and out the door.

Seeing no evidence of the creature he might be dealing with, the ranger moved on to look through the window of another house. It was almost identical. Blood. Debris. The door forced in. Again, the smears on the floor were proof that wounded people had been dragged from their homes.

Crossing the street, Asher approached what appeared to be some kind of shop—a butcher's perhaps. The hooks were swinging in the wind, absent any meat, and the door hung at an angle from one of its hinges. There was no one inside, not even a body, be it human or animal. Like the houses across the street, there were signs of a struggle and blood smeared across the floor.

Asher's suspicions were beginning to grow.

He consulted A Chronicle of Monsters: A Ranger's Archive, its pages clear in his mind. There were a few monsters that might have been assigned to the kind of massacre he was investigating, but he had a feeling he was hunting a monster not found in those archives.

Coming to a stop in the middle of the village's only crossroads, Asher took in the largest building in all of Hogstead. The tavern had no name nor need of one. The name *Felick* came to mind, conjured from deep memory. The owner would be long dead by now, he reasoned, taken by old age if he had any luck.

Looking left and right at the crossroads, where he could see the other invaded homes and shops, Asher listened to his hunch and crouched again. Drawing his short-sword, the ranger sliced down through the snow and shifted it to one side. He found what he was looking for but continued to move more snow aside, widening his search area.

Rising once more, he looked down on intersecting lines of frozen blood. From every street and home, those thick smears came to a single point at the tavern's door.

Taking a step back, the ranger examined the building, paying closer attention to its windows and roof. The latter was covered in snow and the former were boarded up from the inside.

He didn't need to see through the windows, of course, his blood beginning to boil. He already knew what he would find therein.

Thinking about the space he would have inside, Asher kept the short-sword in hand and strode towards the tavern's entrance. His right boot came up and slammed into the door, breaking the lock and twisting the hinges, taking the door clean from sight.

The smell struck him first.

Death had its own kind of odour, a putrid and rancid scent that promised never to fade in memory. The stench was that and more, the tavern assaulted by additional smells. Rot. Mould. It would have been enough to turn even the most hardened of warriors away, but Asher had to see it for himself.

The sky's pale light was enough to banish some of the shadows inside and allow the ranger to place the bare bones of the large room in memory. The hearth in the centre was cold, its flames long left to die. Beyond it, the bar stretched from one wall to the other, though it did not display any drinks, tankards, or the usual sundries often seen on the shelves in most taverns.

Instead, it was lined from end to end with severed heads.

They filled the shelves and spilled onto the bar, each placed ear to ear. Streaked with blood, their every face was stretched in agony, their final moments a torment. Another step and his boot nudged something on the floor. Asher narrowed his eyes, trying to make sense of the body part he was looking at.

It was a forearm, he decided. Snapped at the elbow with every finger and thumb bitten off the hand. It was one of many body parts littering the tavern floor. Like the forearm, every torn limb or torso was in pieces, the flesh stripped and devoured.

Asher had no doubt that all of Hogstead filled the tavern, their bodies brought together where they could be feasted on in the dark. The ranger knew immediately what manner of beast he was hunting, just as he knew he wasn't the only one drawing breath inside that frigid room.

With his free hand, Asher reached out both physically and ethereally. He could feel it, that intangible veil finer than parchment, finer than a single strand of silky hair. The ranger had only to touch it in his mind, and the realm of magic would flow through him, his body a conduit to that inexplicable world.

From the palm of his hand he birthed an orb of light, the globule rising from his skin to float up towards the angled ceiling. His eyes slowly tracked up, careful not to look directly at the orb itself.

Two dozen eyes, surely as black as the pits of hell, looked down at him. *Orcs.*

The first of their wretched kind to leap at him fell upon the orb, extinguishing it.

Asher sidestepped, his sword arm flicking up and across to slice neatly through the orc's waist. By the time it slammed into the floor it was almost severed completely in half, its dark and vile blood adding to the rest.

It rained monsters after that, their roars a deafening cacophony. The timbers creaked in relief and the floor thundered under their collective impact. While short in length, the silvyr blade cut left then right, removing the arm of one before splitting another's face down the middle.

Their numbers brought a degree of chaos to the tavern, with most turning violent on the orc beside them in order to reach the fresh meat that had invaded their nest. Of those who came for Asher, they were met by precision and skill, both of which were supported by a blade that knew no equal among their smiths.

Always, the ranger would find the exposed areas where a simple knick would open an artery or a quick stab would puncture something vital. The floor was soon slick with orc blood and all the harder to navigate with the growing number of body parts.

Asher's attempt to evade an incoming axe saw his right leg skid, breaking his stance. Changing his strategy, the ranger simply dropped to one knee, allowing the axe to pass harmlessly over his head, and thrust the short-sword up into the orc's pale gut.

With a roar of his own, he powered forwards, ramming the dying fiend into those behind it. There was one among them, however, who would not be budged. The orc stood a head taller than its kin, its hands as big as Asher's face. There was no time to swing before it picked him up by belt and throat. The floor taken from beneath his feet, the ranger was thrown across the tavern, over the hearth, and into a pile of broken corpses.

Most of the orcs hesitated to cross the soft beam of light that cut across the middle of the room, where the doorway exposed the tavern to the outside world. The big one didn't hesitate. With a growl, it leaped through the light, scooping up a fallen sword on the way.

It didn't matter.

Asher had decided the orc would be dead before its feet touched the floor, and so it was.

There was no telling whether the orc registered the flash of silvyr as it flew from the ranger's hand, but its twisted expression in death suggested a notch of pain had been delivered as the blade ploughed through its chest mid-air.

There followed a moment of inaction, the remaining orcs reassessing the human.

If only they knew.

Asher rose, his hand reaching for the broadsword on his hip when the beasts found their courage. As one, they charged through the corridor of light, braving the *sky fire*, to avenge their fallen.

Instinct forced the ranger's hand up, his innate magic exploding from his palm in a crushing wave of compressed air. The closest orcs were hammered by that wave and launched in the opposite direction with a collection of shattered bones.

The air was cleaved by the ring of silvyr, his broadsword freed at last. Meeting the rest of the orcs with a charge of his own, the ranger sprung with his final step and came down with a two-handed swing. There was no flesh that could stand against silvyr, not even the stone-like slabs of orcish muscle. That single swing decapitated one and bore down through shoulder to chest of another.

Catching the glint of steel, Asher adjusted his grip on the hilt and spun the blade to deflect a sword before deftly spinning it the other way to block an axe. A swift boot to the chest pushed the sword-wielding orc back, giving him the space to pivot, duck under another cutting axe, and hack through the midriff of a third.

Still, their number combined with the confined space, slick floor, and strewn body parts was against the ranger. He felt the bite of a sword slice through his left thigh and a hammer blow to his right hip. It was enough to stagger him, causing him to miss the knotted fist that struck him across the jaw.

The next thing he knew, Asher was on his back and lying in the snow. He felt the wind wash over him, a welcome balm against the heat and musk of the tavern.

The ranger sat up with no real urgency—he wasn't in danger anymore. The fools had knocked him into the light of day, well beyond their twisted idea of courage. They crowded around the edges of the doorway, peeking out here and there.

He rubbed his jaw, feeling the sting where the skin had been cut. It had been a while since he had taken a straight hit from an orc. He had forgotten how hard they could punch.

As the ranger began to rise, a shadow drifted over the village. He looked up, sure of what he would see, only to be surprised by the dark clouds pushing their way east, shrugged free of The Vengoran Mountains' great shoulders.

The crunch of snow found his ears.

Returning his gaze to the tavern, one of the orcs had stepped beyond the threshold. Its foul eyes squinted at the dull light but they soon adjusted, widening in revelation as they settled on Asher once more.

In its wake, two more followed, each raising a hand to shield against the clouded sky. They too found the light bearable, their weapons gripped all the tighter in their other hand.

Asher swore under his breath.

They flooded the village crossroad, spilling out of the tavern at speed.

And they were not all. From huts and buildings on the surrounding streets, orcs broke free of their dwellings and honed in on the distinct scent of human flesh. It wasn't just a hunting party. It was an entire horde.

Typical of their kind, they wore no armour, their muscled torsos on display. They were nearly as pale as the snow, their skin mottled and marred by cracks, as if crafted from stone. Each had their own crown of horns, the rugged bone of unique shape and size for every one of them.

Passively, Asher scanned those rushing towards him, searching for any sign of the black flame upon their bare chests, marking them as the Sons of Karakulak, that once dreaded and powerful orc. Those of his kin had been seen to brave the light of day, increasing the threat they posed. None bore the mark of that tribe, however, presenting a dark development for all orc-kind.

Scrutinising the orcs was not his only reason for standing idly in the snow. The Realm of Magic flowed through him, his very bones a conduit between the two worlds. As the orcs had piled upon the snowy ground, Asher had been drawing on that immense power, summoning it into the palm of his hand. Concealed by the edge of his cloak, the beasts failed to see the glow of his fingers, the light desperate to be unleashed.

Keeping the broadsword by his side, the ranger thrust out his hand and slaughtered the orcs in droves. The light was so intense that most were blinded before the force of the magic slammed into their bodies, crushing their bones and scorching their skin.

The light vanished the moment he clenched his fist.

The earth was black, littered with unrecognisable corpses.

Asher stared at his hand, smoke rising from the skin. He had never used such magic before and knew it had come from his rage, from his disgust at what the orcs had done to Hogstead. He also couldn't feel his hand it was so numb.

The ranger's display of magic, however, was not enough to dissuade the surviving orcs from exacting vengeance on him. What was left of their horde—who could still see after the intense light—came for his blood.

Breaking into a dead run, the ranger cut between two houses, leaping over a cart, to dash across the next street. Their growls and roars followed him, hounded him through the shell of a village. He turned left and right, only doubling back where he knew he could barrel through a back door and ram his way out through the other side.

Arrows inevitably followed him, whistling passed his head or *thudding* into the wooden buildings around him.

Sighting the trio of archers, Asher skidded to a stop and clenched his fist in front of his face, calling again on his magic. The near-invisible shield repelled all three arrows in a spatter of multi-coloured light. The ranger's hand shot out, his instincts driving his command of magic, and the trio were flung at speed into the building behind them.

Aware of those rushing him from behind, Asher pivoted and brought forth even more magic, basking in the power it granted him.

How seducing it was, to wield such a weapon with his fingertips alone. The incoming orcs were exposed to another bout of raw magic, the light and strength of it ripping them to pieces, along with the huts either side.

The numbness began to grow. While he could still lift his left arm, he could no longer bend the elbow. Yet there was more magic beyond the veil—he could feel it. Infinite power. More than anything he wanted to open himself entirely to the flow of magic and let it rush out of him like the sun. It would wipe them out, he knew. All of them. There would be nothing left of Hogstead, not even a trace that the orcs had attacked.

What power...

There came a warning voice in the back of his mind. It made the ranger hesitate.

Raw magic was dangerous.

It came with consequences.

The moment was broken by the orcs, who called after him in their wicked speech, taunting him, promising him a slow and painful end. How bold they grew when they thought themselves the hunter and not the prey.

But it was not so.

Leaving his magic where it was, for now, the ranger took to fleeing again, though his efforts were quite deliberate. He had given the horde a chance to bunch together in their pursuit, their number now collected at the crossroad again.

Asher skidded to a halt and turned to face them, his silvyr broadsword held high in his good hand as if he meant to fight them all. He had no such intention, of course, lowering his weapon and adopting a casual stance that confused the mass of orcs. All too late did they see the *real* predator.

Have you had your fun? came the familiar voice in the back of his mind, like honey for the soul.

Your turn, Asher replied across their bond.

The shrieks and screams of the frightened orcs were entirely drowned out by the roar of fire, the insatiable flames spat forth from an indomitable dragon.

It was blinding too, forcing the ranger to turn his head, and the heat was such that he raised his free hand, fist clenched, and built a near-invisible shield that arced around him. It flared and protested as the fire lanced at it and the orcs careened into it, burning from head to toe.

Avandriell rose over them as she landed in the heart of Hogstead, her size and long tail causing as much destruction as her breath. In the light of her flames, the dragon's scales shone in all their beauty, a bronze unlike any found in the earth. The spines along her back were dull, the bones flat and rounded as they were on all females. As if to mark her royal lineage, the three horns upon her head were broad and strong, a crown befitting of a dragon. With golden eyes she surveyed her work and with glee she watched the survivors flee, scattering through the village.

Well aware that his companion had deliberately spared some from the flames, Asher calmly returned to the tavern and retrieved his silvyr short-sword, sliding the blade from the dead orc's chest. The mayhem outside was just as he had left it, the smell of smoking flesh staining the air. He made his way to the western edge of Hogstead, content to wait.

Avandriell was always a sight to behold, but even more so when she was given free rein to bring utter ruin upon her enemy.

The dragon crushed the burning and charred bodies under foot as she stalked after her pale prey. All the speed two legs could offer would never be enough to outpace a dragon at a brisk walk.

Avandriell stormed through the village, ploughing through the empty buildings as if they weren't even there. Her jaws open, she would snatch at the running orcs and grind them to pulp and broken bones before spitting them out. A single swipe of her claws was enough to end them, their foul bodies separated into bloody pieces.

Those who fled her jaws found no escape, blind to the powerful tail that swept through Hogstead. Snow, wood, and all manner of debris was kicked into the air before the dragon's tail clubbed or impaled the orcs, throwing them far and wide. In less than a minute since her arrival, there was no Hogstead left, save a single building to Asher's left. It was to be a grave now.

The last of the orcs was clamped in Avandriell's maw and tossed high into the air, so it might see its fate on the way down. The beast's cry was silenced the moment her jaws snapped shut.

The taste of orc is bad enough, she complained, spitting it out. *I shall not add its bitter ilk to my body.*

Asher sheathed his broadsword and sighed. He would be lying if he denied his love for the hunt or the slaying of orcs, he only wished it hadn't come at the expense of Hogstead. They were good folk trying to scratch out a living in the coldest of places. Now it was gone forever, wiped from Illian's lands.

You should never unleash your magic like that, the dragon chastised. *Our bond allows a great amount of magic to flow through you, but conduits can burn up.*

I didn't, Asher reminded her, not to be lectured on something that didn't even happen.

You thought about it, she intoned, before her head whipped to the south, her nostrils exhaling sharply. *One yet lives,* she reported, sharing some of Asher's righteous anger.

No words were needed to give the dragon pause, her companion's intentions felt through their bond. Asher navigated the debris until he was standing over the half-dead orc. It was coughing up blood, adding to the pool that oozed from his severed arm. Most of its right side was burned black, a portion of its trousers still alight with flames.

The fiend is intact, Avandriell stated.

Asher looked up, meeting her golden eyes.

Mostly, the dragon conceded.

The ranger drew his broadsword again. *Mostly* would do.

2

THE SUMMONS

With all the ceremony it deserved, the orc's head tumbled across the hewn stone, tossed carelessly from the ranger's hand.

It came to a stop at the foot of Lord Gantry's humble throne, where all in attendance could look in horror. He patted the air, bidding his advisors and local highborns be quiet, his own expression soured in disgust.

"An *orc*, my Lord," Asher declared, sure that the rich and privileged of Longdale had never seen the likes of such a creature.

"This is most troubling," the lord admitted, rising to approach the severed head. "Orcs have never been seen this far east of The Iron Valley. Hogstead?"

Asher held the room in silence for a moment, if out of respect for the dead. "Gone, my Lord. The village was wiped out."

The lord of Longdale lowered his head, fists clenched. "As I feared."

"There's more," Asher said, his eyes catching Gantry before shifting to the onlookers.

"I should like to conclude my business with the ranger in *private*," Lord Gantry announced.

Longdale's most powerful and wealthiest inhabitants shuffled out of the grand chamber, each sparing Asher a glance.

Their bloodlines will speak of this day for generations.

Avandriell's words were so close as to be his own thoughts, though he could *feel* the bronze dragon gliding a mile over his head.

The day they met the legendary Asher, she continued, her tone almost genuine, *the man death could not contain.*

Don't forget about his legendary mount, Asher dared to jest.

The dragon bristled. *Do I look like a horse, mud-walker?*

"*More* troubling?" Lord Gantry queried, as the doors shut behind the last of his guests.

"While clouded," Asher described, "the light of day was such that no orc would tolerate its touch. Yet they did," he reported gravely.

Lord Gantry's head twitched, his eyes darting from the ranger to the severed head in the middle of his hall. "Truly?"

"There have been rumours since the end of the war that orcs from the Sons of Karakulak can brave the sun," Asher explained, "but the orcs who attacked Hogstead hailed from a different tribe."

The muscles inside Gantry's jaw tensed, a flash of anger rearing its head. "I trust you slaughtered them all."

Asher hesitated, displeased with the lord's choice of words where his actions were concerned.

"None survived," he stated, phrasing it his own way. "But it was more than a scouting party. Their numbers were that of a *raiding horde*. The rest of their tribe is more than likely in the hills around Hogstead. If not there, then they await news in the shadows of the mountain somewhere. I would send word to Namdhor at once. It begs further investigation."

"I'll say," Lord Gantry agreed, reaching for his goblet. "Orcs braving the sun. Decimating entire villages. What's next? Should I prepare Longdale for invasion?"

Detecting a note of hyperbole, Asher gripped the buckle of his belt in both hands, though his left hand was still so numb as to barely feel the cold iron.

"I can't speak to that, my Lord. I'm just a ranger."

Gantry looked over his goblet, disbelief in his eyes. "There's nothing *just* about you, Asher. Your name carries like the wind from here to The Arid Lands. There's not a soul in the realm who doesn't know of your part in The Fated War. Or The Ash War," he added as an afterthought. "Or The War for the Realm, in fact."

It was with Avandriell's aid that Asher controlled the flood of memories that sought to overwhelm him. It was all there at his fingertips now. Every splatter of blood and flash of steel. Every cry of death and sting of loss. Through their bond, his memories had crystallised, dredging up his every waking moment even before Avandriell hatched.

And damned if most of his life hadn't been fighting in one war or another...

"Be that as it may, my Lord, it's not my place to speak on such matters. Avandriell and I are rangers—we're in the business of monsters. I'm sure Queen Inara can spare a few Guardians of the Realm to investigate further."

"The Guardians of the Realm travel in *pairs*," Lord Gantry pointed out. "I need a battalion if they are to comb the hills around Hogstead."

Asher did his best not to take the rejection as an insult to Inara, their commander and instructor.

"They are formidable warriors all, my Lord," he replied tactfully. "And more proof of orc movements will be required if battalions are to be re-tasked."

"More proof than *your* word?" Gantry asked, closing the gap between them.

"My *assumptions*," Asher was sure to specify.

The lord of Longdale probed the decapitated head with the tip of his boot so he might peer at the severed throat.

"Very well. Perhaps you could ask Her Grace to send the very best from their ranks then. The threat of orcs should be taken seriously."

Avandriell bristled again.

We are not his messengers, she fumed.

"Forgive me," Gantry entreated, seeing a hint of confusion cross the ranger's face. "I get ahead of myself. You must also forgive my lack of recall. It was months ago now, and I should have informed you upon your arrival, but my fear for the people of Hogstead was a distraction, and justified apparently."

"My Lord?"

"Runners were dispatched to every city back in the spring. Word from the *king*. Your presence is requested in Namdhor."

Asher glanced at the banner on the wall above the banquet table, where the flaming sword reminded all who held the real power in Illian. He then looked expectantly at the lord, waiting on the rest of the message, when it dawned on him that there wasn't anymore message to give.

"Then I shall leave for Namdhor," he said simply, bowing his head.

"Not before I pay you, I hope," Lord Gantry replied, calling for one of his servants beyond the main hall. "I don't want to be known as the lord who didn't pay his ranger's fee."

Asher accepted the small chest from the servant. By the weight of it, he guessed the lord of Longdale had overpaid. He wouldn't be the first in a position of power to give more than agreed, believing that they were endearing themselves to the legendary ranger. He had since learned how to manage the situation.

"Our business is concluded," he stated, making to leave. "I will speak to the queen on the matter of the orcs, my Lord. I have no doubt the response will be swift."

"I hope you're right," Gantry told him. "You know better than most the ruin even a single orc can cause."

While brief, Asher relived a few seconds on the battlefield, beyond Namdhor. He was surrounded by snarling orcs and the clamour of war, the sound of it all drowned out by the roar of Karakulak, their beast of a king. The wretch had personally slain dragons and murdered Dragorn, revelling in their immortal blood.

Yes. He knew well the ruin of orcs.

"My Lord," he said by way of farewell.

With the chest tucked under one arm, the ranger departed the main hall and worked his way through the streets of Longdale. Built in the skeleton of an ancient dwarven mining town, its outer wall arched around the city proper and cleaved to the Vengoran rock. While the city had grown well beyond the original site, there was evidence almost everywhere of dwarven architecture, the design adopted by the human inhabitants centuries earlier.

Asher was sure to make a detour on his way out, his extended path taking him through the most impoverished district in Longdale. Stray dogs and cats dashed about nearly as much as the children did, and all between failing businesses and run-down markets.

It has been twenty years, Avandriell said into his mind, *and yet we are still treated like Dragon Riders, or worse—Dragorn!*

You know that isn't true.

We are summoned by House Draqaro, the dragon argued. *Such were the Riders of old!*

Asher dipped into an alley and began to ascend the two-storey building at speed, tossing the chest up ahead of him before he was halfway. Wandering over the tops of the district, he opened the chest lid and began grabbing coins. Handful after handful, he released them into the streets below. Some were found immediately by passersby, while the rest would be found in time, and likely by the children who played in the snow.

It's not a summons, it's a request, Asher reminded her.

There is no difference when issued from royalty.

Asher thought back to what had proved a pivotal moment in his life, when he had met Nathaniel Galfrey and his ward, Elaith. It had been another life, he knew, and literally so given his death in between.

As a ranger I have accepted summons from kings and queens before, he told her.

While Avandriell knew this to be true, gleaning as much from his memories, the dragon still took umbrage with the message, her feelings lighting up the bond between them.

If it helps, Asher suggested, putting the last handful of coins into a pouch on his belt, *think of the longhorn cattle that graze along The King's Lake.*

Somewhere above him, where the low clouds drifted lazily over the mountains, a dragon felt a pang of hunger she couldn't ignore.

3

THE HOUSE OF
THE FLAMING SWORD

It had been twenty years since that fateful day. Twenty years since the ranger had touched the sky astride Avandriell for the very first time. It was still the greatest feeling in all the world, as if the very notion of freedom was a tangible thing he could reach out and grasp with both hands. The world had lost its limits, shrinking about him while also seen to be unimaginably vast from the heavens.

So too did that feeling soar in Avandriell's heart. Was there ever a creature so content as a dragon in flight, and made all the more whole by their companion? Every facet of her bronze scales shone under the afternoon sun, a jewel in the sky yet a predator to all beneath.

Nestled comfortably in his saddle, Asher probed their bond, getting a sense of where her mind had drifted to. As she often would while skimming the clouds beneath her, Avandriell dwelled on ancient times, memories passed down from her mother, Thessaleia. On the periphery of their bond, the ranger could hear some of those memories playing out.

Your mother was a formidable dragon, he said, feeling some of Avandriell's admiration. There was also grief, he felt, a sadness that they would never meet her.

She would have liked you, the dragon commented. *Her Rider was like you. Our bond feels an echo of theirs.*

Perhaps that's why we bonded, Asher posed.

In part, Avandriell accepted. *But our bond is our own. We were always meant to find each other. An unfortunate series of events for the monsters of the world,* she added mischievously.

Asher patted her scales beyond his saddle. Every waking moment was a dream with Avandriell, his life having turned in a direction he couldn't have hoped for. How long had he walked hand-in-hand with Death, his own assured at the end of that road? To be immortal and accompanied by a creature so magnificent as Avandriell was an endless journey, the destination inconsequential.

We're here, she informed him. *Are you ready?*

Asher frowned.

Am I ready? You make it sound as if we're going into battle.

We might be, the dragon remarked. *All too often are we considered an extension of the flaming sword. We are neither weapon nor shield of House Draqaro. We are rangers. Our lives are our own and our skills come at a price.*

Asher chuckled silently to himself.

You and I both know that if House Draqaro comes under threat, we will be on the front line.

Not necessarily.

Wait until you see Adilandra, the ranger said, a smile edging on his lips as he conjured his last memory of the young princess. *You always melt when you see her.*

Avandriell threw her head back. *I do not melt.*

You melt, Asher repeated. *Like ice on a hot day.*

Without warning, the bronze dragon tucked in her wings and dived, punching through the clouds like a spear. Asher managed to grip the reins a little tighter, his knuckles paling, but he was still parted from his saddle for a time.

When, at last, she levelled out and he returned to his seat, the ranger took a much needed breath and released the spell that had been keeping him warm, the bubble dissipating without sight or sound.

You did that on purpose.

Avandriell exhaled sharply through her nostrils and dipped her head, taking them down at a steady rate.

There beneath them, the capital of Illian rose up from the ground, a monument to human civilisation and ingenuity. Like a small ocean, The King's Lake dominated everything north and south of the city, its mirrored surface disappearing into a haze beyond sight. Namdhor itself sat proud upon the mighty rock that angled up over the lake, its collection of towers, spires, and cathedrals mounting to the keep at its apex.

The Dragon Keep.

Home to the Draqaros, the keep had seen much of what would become history, tales that would survive to the end of time.

Asher himself had more than a few memories from atop its dark stone. It seemed an odd thing, to have memories so vile as trying to assassinate Alijah Galfrey to memories so beautiful as the wedding between Vighon and Inara.

After sweeping over the city once, Avandriell circled back and glided down to the lower village that sprawled across Namdhor's base.

What are you doing? Asher asked. *The Keep's at the top of the hill.*

I am aware, the dragon replied, her claws settling into the muddy path that cut between the village and up through the heart of the city. *It's good that the people get to see us.*

The ranger sighed. *I hate it when you do this.*

I love it! came her gleeful response.

As they would, the people of Namdhor rushed from their lives to line the road and stare at the magnificent dragon. And what a sight she was. A daughter of Garganafan, one of the largest dragons to have ever graced earth and sky, Avandriell was already larger than most of her kin. As such, the ground shook beneath her feet, her steady pace taking them up the city's incline.

Those born since The Fated War, who had not witnessed the hatred brought against the world by Malliath and Alijah, ran alongside Avandriell, looking upon the heroes oft heard in song and ballads.

Then there were those who had lived through the occupation, when armoured Darklings had patrolled the streets, reducing the people's freedom while hunting down any and all who felt a connection to the realm of magic. They were older now, weathered by time and a violent youth.

Older still were those who had lived through The Ash War, nearly forty years ago. They had stood shoulder to shoulder, sword and shield brought to bear in defence of Namdhor and all the realm. They were true survivors and all worthy of the title *hero*. Their grit and sacrifices had kept the orcs at bay, making the capital the last bastion of man and hope for a time. Asher respected them all.

It seemed an age for the ranger, who had all the ages yet to come, before they arrived at The Dragon Keep. Avandriell had soaked up every second of praise, her head held high and tail extended. Asher jumped down, his right hand running over his companion's smooth scales before his boots touched down.

Now, if you'll excuse me, Avandriell said, her wings unfurling, *my presence is required elsewhere.*

Enjoy the Longhorn.

Asher watched her flap those mighty wings and leave Namdhor behind, his green cloak swept out in the sudden gust.

While every neck was craned and every set of eyes trailed Avandriell's ascent, the ranger made for the main gates before he could be harangued.

In the years since he bonded with a dragon, he had discovered a number of myths the people attached to Riders. Some believed that his touch alone would heal them of ailments, while others believed that his blessing would bring good fortune. Then there were the marriage proposals, the young women placed in his path by eager parents.

25

Arriving on dragon back, however, did have its advantages. The guards at the gate bowed their heads and cleared his path into the keep. Gone were the days of bartering or sneaking in, his status as a ranger forgotten in the shadow of Avandriell.

The courtyard was slow to resume its activities, the servants brought to a standstill by the dragon in flight. Asher weaved through, avoiding the horse being taken back to the stables and strode towards the keep doors.

"Halt!" barked the sharp command, bringing the ranger to a stop.

The tip of a blade came to rest on his pauldron of bronze dragon scales.

"I'll not suffer a scoundrel in my home," the young voice stated.

Asher looked back over one shoulder. "What did I always tell you?" he asked, doing his best to withhold his smile. "If you're to ever free your sword, be prepared to *use* it."

The ranger pivoted, the steel dragging harmlessly over the scales until he was free of it. At the same time, his right arm whipped up, bringing his broadsword with it, the silvyr unleashed in the frigid air. He now pointed it at Prince Athis, the first-born and only son of House Draqaro. With twenty winters behind him, he had filled out into his father's frame, his muscles defined beneath his shirt. His hair fell in raven locks, better tended to than Vighon's had ever been, but he possessed his mother's blue eyes, each a drop stolen from the richest of oceans.

He was also a quarter elf, a fact that made him just a notch stronger and faster than his peers. He used both to spring and lash out at the ranger, his sword rolling in his grip. Asher was careful to block both strikes without causing too much damage to the prince's steel. The technique, he knew, was to deflect rather than allow the swords to meet edge to edge.

"Your footwork has improved," Asher complimented, their duel taking them across the courtyard.

"You've been gone for three years," Athis replied, feigning his thrust only to swing horizontally. "I vowed to draw blood when next we sparred."

He had certainly been practising. Asher saw flashes of Inara's technique—a deadly form of combat—with an underlying style adopted from Vighon—a form of combat all his own.

The ranger batted the prince's sword aside and kicked his inside foot, knocking him off balance enough that a slight shove put him on his back. "I said *improved*. I didn't say it was any *good*."

Somewhere between amusement and embarrassment, Athis jumped to his feet and returned to the fight with abandon. Asher moved his limbs and shifted his stance and shoulders more than anything, his sword left in reserve. They had the attention of all, of course, the servants and guards alike rooted to the spot.

"Perhaps you fancy yourself a Guardian of the Realm," Asher taunted. "They could do with having someone around to shine their boots."

His wild grin only enflamed the prince's bruised ego all the more. The ranger saw his attack coming a mile off. He twisted the silvyr in his hand, rolling the incoming steel away, before hitting the young man with the flat of the blade, forcing him onto his tiptoes.

"Are you so quick to forget my lessons, boy?" Asher slowly rounded on his opponent, sword held low at his side. "Emotions have their time and place. Use them to gauge right from wrong and then put them to one side."

"I suppose you've never been swayed by your emotions in battle."

The new and considerably fairer voice took the fight right out of Asher, turning him towards the keep's doors.

There she stood, the *original* Guardian of the Realm. Formerly Galfrey, Inara Draqaro was a warrior-queen incarnate, ever strong, her wit as sharp as her Vi'tari blade. Cutting was the slightest of smirks that thinned her lips, her words biting through to the truth of things.

"Your Grace," Asher greeted warmly, bowing his head.

"Perhaps you would like to duel with me next?" she enquired lightly, her hand falling to rest on the crystalline pommel of her scimitar.

"I would never be so bold, Your Grace," the ranger replied, sheathing his sword. "Nor so *foolish*."

Inara let her true smile beam through before crashing into him with a powerful embrace. Her mother's strength still lingered in her veins, even if her immortality did not. To that end, Asher noted a few more grey strands paling her dark hair, her eyes crowned in the same hard lines that pulled at her lips. Though time had done naught to diminish the woman, it still bruised the ranger's heart to see her age, to know that a day was coming that would darken all the days thereafter.

Upon her breast, kept there by a fine chain, was a single dragon scale of deepest red. Athis—the prince's namesake—would forever be imprinted on the ranger's mind, his sacrifice an example of how the light would always overcome the dark.

"You have been missed," she said for him alone.

Asher squeezed her a little tighter. "I only came to see the little one," he quipped.

Inara pulled back from him. "She is not so little."

"Asher!" His name was declared with glee and excitement, as ever from Illian's only princess.

The ranger moved aside so he might see the daughter of House Draqaro. It took him a moment to reconcile with the girl he had last seen three years ago, and the tall lithe girl that bounded up to him. From four to seven, Adilandra had grown, seemingly more aware of her limbs. Given her size, it felt wrong to scoop her up, and so he held her close, the girl's head falling just short of his chest.

"Where's Ava?" she asked desperately.

Asher glanced at the sky. "Never come between a dragon and her next meal," he told her.

Three more years of life hadn't stopped the girl from pouting. "I want to see her."

"Soon," he promised. "You won't be able to keep her away."

"Why have you returned?" Adilandra asked bluntly, her decorum still hindered by youth.

"That's a very good question, Princess." Asher looked to Inara expectantly.

"Did you bring me anything?" Adilandra asked outright, her mother too slow to respond.

Asher made a look of sizing her up. "I might have a dagger on my saddle just right for you—"

"No," Inara interjected, drawing the short word out.

"Made by the finest blacksmith in Ameeraska," Asher added.

"Still no."

Adilandra whined as her mother guided her towards the doors. Athis made no move to follow them, speaking of friends he intended to visit and a promise to return before sunset.

"Girls," Inara whispered with a coy smile. "Be sure to join us at the campsite," she instructed.

"I'll have that drop of blood, Ranger," the prince called back.

Asher glanced at his scaled pauldron, noting the nick in the supporting material. "You'll have to settle for scratching my leathers, boy."

Turning back, he let his eyes roam over The Dragon Keep, a fortress he had infiltrated once upon a time. As he did, he felt his bond with Avandriell steadily diminishing, soon to be shut off completely by the dragon herself. She had spotted the Longhorns then. Ever the predator, Avandriell was honing in on her prey. What would inevitably follow wasn't something Asher needed, or wanted, to share with her.

"How long has it been since you rode?" Inara asked, looking to the stables.

Asher's lips parted with what he thought would be an easy answer, yet the number of years escaped him.

"Why?" he asked instead.

"Vighon isn't here," the queen informed him. "Even after all these years, there's only so much of royal life he can endure. He hates being waited on all the time." Inara jutted her chin to the north. "He's taken himself off to the other side of The King's Lake. He had a campsite built there some years ago. It serves as an ample retreat. I'm sure you, yourself, would enjoy it more than this ancient stone."

"I suppose I would," Asher replied with a smile.

Inara beamed. "Then we ride."

The queen was swift with her commands, ensuring that Adilandra was taken care of and reassured that she would join them by the lake at sunset. All the while, two horses were being saddled and made ready, along with a pair of guards, their cuirasses and cloaks displaying the flaming sword.

Asher did his best to fall on muscle memory as he climbed up the shire horse. His thoughts drifted back through the years, recalling Hector, his first horse. It seemed another life.

Seen to by a pair of handmaidens, Adilandra was clearly torn between her duty as a young princess, a duty that demanded a certain level of decorum, and her feelings as a seven year-old girl who adored the ranger. Still, she managed a smile and waved at Asher as she made for the keep doors.

The ranger's own smile was somewhat strained, the taste of iron on his tongue—*blood*. He closed off the last of his bond with Avandriell before her fangs sank any deeper into cow flesh.

"Where have you come from?" Inara enquired, guiding her horse into line beside his.

"Longdale," he informed her, glimpsing the red snows of Hogstead in his mind. As they descended Namdhor's slope, the ranger went on to report his findings there and the subsequent conversation with Lord Gantry. The queen was saddened at news of Hogstead's demise, her demeanour souring all the more to know that orcs were the cause of the massacre.

"I will have the Guardians look into it immediately," she assured.

Having put the city behind them, they rounded the lower village and turned back on themselves, trotting towards the lake shore. Asher did his best to appear comfortable aside the horse, but damned if it wasn't unpleasant. He had forgotten about the rhythm of riding, the constant impact, and—worst of all—lack of clear communication with the creature upon which he rode. It was worth it to ride with Inara though, the once Dragorn as captivating as a person could be.

With the guards on their flank, they began the long journey around the lake's edge, its surface yet to harden in early winter. The ranger was confronted by yet more memories, his life having taken him almost everywhere. Thanks to his bond with Avandriell, it seemed only yesterday he entered the depths of the lake in search of the Golem, Sir Borin the Dread.

With hours still ahead of them, Asher was most pleased when a familiar shadow swept over the shore. The horses reacted accordingly, their hooves gouging through the hard mud to bring them to a halt. They shook their heads, grunting with unease, as the bronze dragon made a tight circle and landed in their path, her wings batting the air.

Asher could feel his companion's amusement at the sight of him, feet hooked into stirrups.

You're going to smell of horse for days, she complained.

The ranger put one finger to his bottom lip. **You have a little cow in your teeth.**

More than aware that she stood before the queen of Illian and the commander of the Guardians, Avandriell worked her jaw to retrieve the strip of flesh and gulp it down.

I would not have you arrive before the king in this manner, the dragon told him, lowering herself in invitation.

Asher looked to Inara beside him. He hesitated, unsure whether extending that invitation was only inviting a degree of heartache. There was no feeling in the world like parting from the earth on dragon back, but it would inevitably remind her of Athis.

"It would be quicker," he simply said.

Whether by emotion or the cold wind, Inara's eyes were glassy as she looked at Avandriell. "It would be an honour," she said, a genuine smile brightening her face.

After handing over the care of the horses to the guards, the pair began their climb up Avandriell's side. Asher stopped himself from offering any aid, the queen ascending with ease and a sense of familiarity.

When situated behind him, her hands wrapped around his waist, the dragon unfurled her wings, their tips flexing high.

Inara gasped, her grip tightening as they launched into the air, a spray of water fanning high to their right. Rather than make for the sky, Avandriell rose no higher than Namdhor's peak upon its rocky rise, her body angling to take them north. Within seconds she had located the campsite and her speed increased. Asher looked over his shoulder to see tears streaking back against Inara's temples. For a short and wonderful time, she was somewhere else, another time.

Deciding the power of her wings alone would upend the camp, the dragon touched down just west of the site, her back legs sinking beneath the water.

"You're just in time!" a voice called out. "The sausages are almost cooked!"

Asher stepped away from Avandriell, rounding one of her mighty wings to locate the source. Standing upon a boulder, casually striking the pose of some antiquated hero, was a northman. Attired in a simple shirt and trousers, he braved the bitter cold with a hungry smile on his face.

Vighon Draqaro.

The son of a crime lord, a fiend who had gained power from oppressing others. The once best friend to the world's most dangerous Dragon Rider, who nearly destroyed the realm of magic. The man who had come from nothing but had everything to give, and give it he did. His deeds had landed a crown on his head and granted him the largest kingdom ever bestowed on a single person.

He was the king of Illian, and it was *his* Age in which they all drew breath.

"Asher!" he damn-near growled, quick to leap from the boulder.

The ranger stopped, unable to advance after the king engulfed him in a tight embrace. "Your Grace," he finally greeted, and with a bow.

Vighon made a face and gestured at their solitude. "It's just us."

Asher gave a tight smile, though a warm one. "It's good to see you, Vighon."

The northman's eyes flitted to his wife. "My love," he said with affection, meeting her with an embrace all of their own. He noted the tears that dampened her skin, leading him to the gargantuan figure of muscle and bronze scales.

"Avandriell," he addressed, bowing in respect.

The dragon dipped her head, pointing all three of her horns to the sky.

I might have hatched for him, she declared slyly.

Asher contorted his smile until it faded, his ego not to be bruised by a playful lie.

"She still prefers me," he said, his voice lacking confidence.

Vighon laughed, patting the ranger's chest. "Of course she does," he replied with a wink. "Come. The sausages will be burning."

The men clapped each other's back and made for the camp.

"Look at you," the northman said, taking him in. "Over a thousand years old and you don't look a day over forty!"

Asher chuckled quietly to himself, musing on his age. He had lost track of the number, struggling to incorporate the thousand years he had spent standing still, trapped in the elven Amber Spell within the ruins of Elethiah. Then there was his actual death in the pools of Naius, after which he had slumbered in numb darkness for thirty years until The Crow used dark magic to resurrect him. The years that had followed were dogged by war, violence, and such bloodshed that they had slipped through recognition.

Either way, the ranger decided, he was *old*.

The man at his side had graced sixty years and managed to retain something of his youth about him. His jaw was still strong beneath his grey beard, and his face, while weathered and scarred, appeared healthy and bright. His hair, silvered with age now, touched his shoulders, though most was tied back on the crown of his head, styled as Asher's was.

It was still easy to see the northman as he had been, a tenacious warrior without equal.

The campsite was nestled on the shore with The Vengoran mountains at its back. Whatever Inara had said of Vighon's feelings for his place on the throne, the camp was certainly fit for a royal family.

It comprised of several tents, a collection that surrounded a great fire pit where the king had been cooking. The largest tent, a rather sturdy pavilion, was set between the roots of the mountain and looked like a library. Its walls had been filled with books, the shelves separated here and there by paintings, blueprints, and various maps.

In the heart of the pavilion there sat a great desk, its polished surface piled with parchments, scrolls, and leather-bound books. A retreat indeed.

"I'm glad our message found you, old friend," he said, one hand guiding Asher by the shoulder. "You're not an easy man to find. You leave tales in your wake but you're never in one place for long."

"Ever is the way of a ranger," Asher replied, sure that Avandriell would have urged him to remind the Draqaros.

"Sometimes I envy you," Vighon admitted. "Come. Let's eat! You must be hungry."

Asher kept himself at the fire's edge, refraining from accepting the offered seat. He glanced back at Avandriell, her anticipation mixing with his own. The message had been a request and they would be friends he held dear in his heart for the rest of his days, but a request from the two most powerful people in the realm was never to be taken lightly.

"Forgive me," he began. "It's just... Avandriell and I are eager to know why we're here."

Vighon's enthusiastic smile lowered into something more serious, if still bright. "Of course. It's us who should ask forgiveness."

"We're just so happy to see you," Inara added, handing the ranger a goblet.

"As are we," Asher assured.

The king put the sausages to one side and wiped his hands down his shirt, rounding the fire as he did. Quite jovially, he gripped the ranger's pauldron and looked him in the eyes.

"We have a monster problem."

4

THE JOB

Asher looked out on the calm waters of The King's Lake, imagining, for a moment, that it might be The Hox. Vast was that ocean, a body of water that could drown the realm were it untethered from its place in the world. And what secrets it kept in its dark depths. What monsters...

"You want us to slay the Leviathan," he said incredulously, still digesting the king's words.

At last, Avandriell proclaimed. *A monster worth my time.*

Leviathans are demons of the deep world, Asher rebutted. **You don't idly challenge one.**

Avandriell's head rose a few metres. *Is that fear I detect in you, Ranger?*

My memories are yours, Asher reminded the dragon, irritation, if not apprehension, creeping into his tone. **You've seen the Leviathan that decimated Dragorn. They're so big they make you look like a mouse—mountains of flesh and claws and fangs and who knows what else.**

Inara and Vighon had both paused, clearly aware that the two were conversing and polite enough to give them the time.

"What is Avandriell saying?" the queen asked.

Asher took a breath. "She's ready to fight that damned thing right now," he relayed miserably.

Avandriell exhaled a sharp jet of air from her nostrils—a strong affirmative.

Vighon licked his lips, the fine muscles in his face twitching with consideration. "I know it's a big job—"

"You didn't see the Leviathan we fought in Dragorn," Asher interjected, one of very few people who could interrupt the king of Illian. "They're not monsters," he went on. "It's too small a word for something capable of wiping out an entire city before breakfast."

"We know from The Crow's research that every Leviathan is different," Inara said calmly. "There's a chance the creature that stalks The Hox is smaller, even weaker, than the one we faced on Dragorn."

Asher's pulse quickened at The Crow's name. Sarkas had brought him back from eternal slumber but the ranger owed him nothing for that second chance, his resurrection marred by the enchantment that enthralled him to Malliath. The terrible things he had done astride that dragon, and all in the name of a bright future brought about by twisted machinations.

Avandriell flooded his mind with a soothing embrace and he welcomed it, allowing her presence to remind him who he was and what he had overcome.

"By that reckoning," he replied to the queen, "there's a chance it's bigger and stronger."

There's only one way to find out, Avandriell intoned.

Asher glanced at his companion, just beyond the camp, before his attention returned to the Draqaros.

"As far as I'm aware," he continued, "that beast has dwelled in those waters for eons. Why does it need dealing with *now?*"

Vighon flicked his head, directing them into the pavilion. Laid into the surface of the desk, carved there by a master craftsman, was a flat and smooth map of Verda. From the east, where the sun graced the day, was Ayda—home to the elves and lands immortal. The heart of the map was taken up by Illian, a united kingdom under the banner of the flaming sword. In the west lay that of Erador, the ancient home of man, and cousins to all of Illian.

"As you know," the northman explained, "it's been three years since Gwenyfer assumed her throne in Erador." He pointed at Valgala, the capital of the west. "With some help from Gideon, she's taken to her duty as best she can, but the realm still has a long way to go before it can return to a time of prosperity."

"Communication between our two thrones has been sparse and unreliable," Inara reported. "At present, our options are few."

Vighon put one finger to Erador's north and arced round, skimming The Dread Wood and into the cold land of Dhenaheim.

"It's a long route on foot and treacherous to boot. If the messengers manage to get past The Dread Wood they face harsh elements."

"It's even worse for caravans and supply trains," Inara added. "They disturb those that should be left to slumber in that wretched wood."

The king nodded in agreement and placed his finger on Erador's eastern coast.

"By sea is quicker, but…" He, again, arced his finger round, following the coast up and back down until he reached Illian. "Because of the Leviathan, all ships have to hug the shore. Jagged and plenty are the fangs of both realms, grounding ships or worse. Any that brave deeper waters never make it. *Never.*"

Inara moved closer and ran a finger in a straight line, connecting Erador to Illian.

"Without the Leviathan, we could set up the very first trade route between our two countries. We could finally bring our two peoples together, to help each other, to strengthen our alliance."

"It would forge a future unlike any that has come before," Vighon proclaimed.

There was a dream behind the king's eyes, a child-like wonder at the world that might be. Asher was pleased to find no trace of greed about the man, nor lust for power or man's greatest weakness—the simple want of *more.* The Draqaros, as ever, only worked for the good of the people under their stewardship. They, if not their dreams alone, were always worth fighting for.

The ranger looked intently at the blank space on the map, the stretch of sea that sat between the two realms of man.

"I would see that future for myself," he said, unable to imagine the size of that new world. "But, truthfully, I have no idea how to go about hunting this thing, never mind killing it. Given how long it's haunted those waters, I'd say no one else does either. I don't know how to bait it. I don't even know what it looks like."

"Surely you've hunted things from the sea before," Vighon remarked.

"Aplenty," Asher confirmed. "But they were monsters that frequented the shore and attacked people. This Leviathan hunts in *deep* waters. Avandriell could fly over it, but the moment it submerges…"

I can fly for days without landing, the dragon insisted.

That won't help you fight a monster ten times your size underwater.

"You're right," Inara replied, holding back a sigh, her hands pressed into the edges of the desk. "We're asking you to kill a famously un-killable monster. But we've been discussing this scenario with Gwenyfer for some time. We've exhausted our options, Asher. Lives were lost just conveying as much."

"What about Gideon and Ilargo?" he posed, they two a natural fit for a mission of import to both realms.

Inara licked her lips, her eyes pinching. "No one knows where Gideon is."

Asher frowned at that. "I thought he was a *Dragon Rider* now. Isn't he sworn to the throne of Erador or such like?"

"He hasn't sworn oaths to any throne," Vighon explained, looking a bit put out.

"The truth is," Inara went on, "we cannot speak to Gideon's intentions. Or his methods. He spoke to us once, a long time ago, about rebuilding the Dragon Riders."

"*A time of Dragon Riders will come again,*" the king voiced, his tone suggesting he was mimicking Gideon verbatim.

Inara moved round the desk to join her husband. "He also said if it took him a hundred years to find even one Rider then so be it. He's being cautious this time. The Dragorn swelled in rank beyond his imagining and, he would be the first to admit, beyond his *experience*. If that's the business he's tending to, he should be left to it."

Not that they could track them if they wanted to, Avandriell remarked, a smug note in her voice.

"Besides," Vighon quipped, leaning against the map, "a legendary monster needs a legendary hunter."

I'm not immune to flattery, Avandriell commented, all for the hunt.

I am, Asher stated.

"Erador and Illian are as one on the matter," Inara continued. "Whatever you need is yours. Resources, manpower, coin. It's yours."

"That's all very well," the ranger agreed, "but what I need is *information*. I can't hunt what I don't know. This thing is no better than a shadow in the water, a footnote in every history book. I'm going to need time to build any kind of understanding about it. How it moves. How it hunts."

"The future we're talking about has to last," Vighon interjected, his tone reassuring. "It can't be built in a day. Every brick has to be carefully laid. You have time, my friend. We don't just want this fiend dead, we want it dead and you and Avandriell returned to us. I know it doesn't need saying, but *do it right*. You're both too valuable to lose."

Those warm words brought out a smile in the ranger. He regarded the map for a time, his thoughts adrift while he considered where to even start such a hunt. He could feel Avandriell's presence, her anticipation building like pressure in the back of his mind.

Think of the bards of the world, the dragon insisted, her tone mixed with excitement and amusement. *They must tire of singing the same songs about us. Let's give them some new material!*

Asher's jaw firmed up, ready to protest such a ridiculous reason to risk their lives. But he relaxed and said nothing of the sort. Instead, he took a breath and raised his head, a quiet smile edging on the corner of his mouth, though it never quite reached his eyes.

"We'll do it."

Vighon brightened at that, his hand coming up to slap the ranger's back. "Then the future is all but set!"

A jet of hot air shot from Avandriell's nostrils, her golden eyes fixed on the tent's interior.

"A problem?" the king enquired.

Asher glanced at his companion. It felt distasteful given what they had discussed and the future for which they all strived, but it was important, he knew, that they recognised them as rangers and not extensions of the flaming sword.

"It's just the matter of our... *fee*," he relayed.

Vighon looked almost embarrassed. "Of course! We would not ask this of you without reward."

Their vision for the world was reward enough, Asher thought, feeling a hint of shame, but hard lines had to be drawn.

"Ask it," the king told him, "and it's yours."

The ranger's lips parted, intending to ask for no more than a single coin, when Avandriell reminded him of a project long overdue. He looked at the map again, reassessing the nature of his fee.

"There is one thing I would ask..."

After detailing his requirements to take on the job, both Vighon and Inara happily accepted, vowing to pay in full and with glad hearts.

"And it might not be much," Inara eventually added, "but if there's any information to be gained, you will find it in Erador. They are more familiar with the beast. To that end, we have already sent someone ahead to begin comprising any and all information on the Leviathan. You will find them here, at Elderhall," the queen reported, pointing to the most eastern city on Erador's shore.

"Who am I looking for?" Asher asked.

Inara smiled knowingly. "An old friend."

5

THE ⊙LD FRIEND

After days of warmth, comfort, and the best of company, Asher found himself on the very edge of Illian's coast, his feet firmly planted on ground south of The Vengoran Mountains. From atop that cliff, the ranger looked out on another world, a realm that always touched his own and sank to depths as unknown as the depths of the heavens above.

The Hox.

The sea had always felt like an invitation to the ranger, a gateway to lands unknown and fortuitous prospects, to a freedom all of its own.

The Hox gave no such invitation.

Under a sheet of grey clouds, its waters were dull, stretching beyond sight. It was a hunting ground and not his own. A shadow of doubt flickered across his thoughts, whispering of a mistake that would cost him everything. It was such times, when his own confidence wavered, that the pillar of strength in his life stood proud.

Avandriell looked over those same waters, her head held high as she took in the many scents that blew in off the sea breeze. Just the sight of her bolstered the ranger's resolve, convincing him that there was nothing they couldn't accomplish together.

If it is for me you fear, the dragon said, speaking softly into his mind, *fear not mud-walker. Should the Leviathan pose a meaningful threat, I can always just… fly away. Can you say the same?* she asked, her humour so wonderfully bleak.

That sounds about right, Asher replied, knowing exactly where the gap in her scales was. **You flying away, leaving me to deal with the monster.**

Avandriell's left claw dug a little deeper into the hard earth.

Asher laughed under his breath and turned away from the vista. "Shall we?" he said aloud, making for his saddle.

Clipping the straps to his belt, he leaned forward and gripped the handles tooled out of the leather, crafted by fine dwarven hands. From the dragon's back, he could only see The Hox between her horns.

Beckoned by the hunt, Avandriell pounced and let herself fall from the edge of the cliff, wings tucked in.

Falling at speed and from such a height was an experience only shared by unfortunate souls who'd ever lost their footing and plummeted to their end. For the immortal ranger, it was a rush unlike any other. The air bombarded him, forcing him to hold his breath until fifteen tons of dragon levelled out. Her scales, each designed by nature to allow the wind to slip right over her body, rippled from the neck down as she angled up into the sky.

Asher closed his eyes, falling back on Gideon's instructions. He imagined the air around him vibrating, clinging to him like a second skin. Before Avandriell pierced the clouds, the ranger was warmed by his magic.

* * *

With but a single stop on the southern shores of the island Carstane—allowing Asher to rest and eat—Avandriell kept to the skies for days as she put watery mile after watery mile behind them. The Hox appeared endless, reaching across the world in every direction, a beast unto itself.

Comfortable though he was in flight, Asher felt a degree of relief upon seeing the hazy line on the horizon. He was a *mud-walker* after all.

Erador was beginning to take shape before his eyes, a land that had known kingdoms when Illian was so young to have known none at all. It was a realm with its own tales and myths, its culture forged from an entirely different history.

Asher recalled his one and only visit, some twenty years ago. Of course, the country's capital, Valgala, was many miles inland and far from sight. That didn't stop him from remembering it in perfect detail. From astride Athis, with Inara and Adan'Karth upon dragon back, he had first laid eyes on Erador's white gem, situated in plains of green, a mighty lake at its heart. Beautiful though it had been, his reason for being in the foreign land conjured ill memories and darker times.

The memory was brightened by Avandriell, who had been waiting for him in Drakanan, slumbering in her egg for untold eons while the world toiled to bring Asher to that very moment. For all the destruction and heart-ache Alijah and Malliath had wrought, the ranger had found his island of peace and harmony.

As Avandriell displayed a stamina worthy of her bloodline, Asher spent the remainder of their long journey dwelling on Adan'Karth. It had been too long since the Drake's name had crossed his mind and, like those who gave their lives to save the realm of magic, the least he deserved was the ranger's thoughts.

And he missed him so…

Using her mother's memory as any would use a map, Avandriell brought them over Erador's soil where she swept over the land, keeping to a south-westerly path across fields of gold and green. For another day they put mile after mile behind them, bringing her distinct shadow over the city of Elderhall.

Nestled inside a lopsided crater, the city was that of a crescent, arcing around the highest walls, where the inhabitants could look down on the sea. The Hox occupied three quarters of the crater, its waters having crept in through a natural gap in the circular wall, allowing for a port to exist on the curved edge of the city. That natural gap had been worked and hewn into a pair of gargantuan statues, each a king with their arm extended as if gesturing at the splendour of Elderhall itself.

Within the waters of its domain there existed a single island, connected to the crescent city via a long bridge. Boasting walls of its own and a collection of spires and domes, Asher assumed it was home to whomever governed Elderhall. Like the rest of the buildings inside the angled crater, the main keep—or perhaps a palace given its beauty and elegance—along with every rooftop on the small island, was a pale red, its walls a stark white.

Avandriell's shadow darkened those tiles, the dragon gliding low from north to south. *My mother's memory doesn't do it justice,* she opined. *It's beautiful...*

The same has been said of you. We should assume Elderhall has fangs of its own and be wary here. We're not in Illian anymore.

There was a sense of excitement in Avandriell, a joy even, to be in the land of her mother. The dragon enjoyed nothing more than a good adventure, though Asher feared such reckless glee came from a simple fact: she had yet to be truly tested. In their twenty years together, neither had faced an opponent capable of threatening death. If the Leviathan was everything the legends said, that was about to change.

Circling the lone island one more time, Avandriell banked to the north and made for a circular courtyard that clung to the shore. While many faces had appeared to watch the bronze dragon come to land, there was an air of caution about the people of Elderhall, an unease that kept them away from the courtyard.

I smell fear, Avandriell reported.

I'm sure Alijah and Malliath left an impression during their reign.

What of Gideon and Ilargo? the dragon asked. *They were here for years fighting war lords and blood barons before Gwenyfer could take the throne.*

Erador is vast. There's every chance these people never saw Gideon and Ilargo. And if they did, Asher went on to pose, **it could have been twenty years ago. Either way, we don't want their fear to spill over into violence. Perhaps you should...**

The dragon gave a subtle shrug of her horned head, a sigh among her kin.

I shall hunt beyond the walls, Avandriell said reluctantly, her companion halfway to the stone under her feet.

The sound of thundering hooves turned Avandriell's head first, leading Asher to the road that curved around the nearest houses, each a block of three storeys that looked to house multiple families. Through their bond, the ranger was notified of all his dragon could smell, hear, and even taste on the air. He knew then that the horses carried men all, and armoured with plate, their swords still sheathed.

But there was another among them, his scent unlike those around him. It was sweeter, lighter even, as if he were no more than a fresh breeze blowing through the cadre around him.

Rounding the houses, seven horses came into view—more importantly, for the mounts, a dragon came into view. All but one braced their legs, coming to a swift halt in sight of those reptilian eyes.

Only the stallion of chestnut brown continued towards them, its fine hairs an almost identical tone to the flowing locks of its rider. All the while they closed the gap, the rider rubbed his horse's neck and whispered into its ear, his words lending the animal a degree of courage in the face of a predator so large as Avandriell.

Such was the power of the *elves.*

"Asher! Avandriell!" the elf called out, a broad grin spitting his chiselled jaw.

The ranger moved to intercept his old friend as the elf glided down from his saddle, his every movement effortless and full of natural grace.

"Galanör!"

The once ranger clapped forearms with Asher before dragging him into a tight embrace. "You are a most welcome sight, my friends!"

Asher glanced beyond the elf, noting the caution that lingered among the soldiers.

"I wouldn't be so sure."

Galanör half turned to regard his previous companions. "Dragon Riders have long been stories of old in these lands. Gideon and Ilargo changed that but, even now, they are more myth than anything. They are yet to learn of your splendour, Avandriell." The elf dropped to one knee and bowed his head before her, one fist clenched to his chest.

Gleaming bronze, Avandriell dipped her head, the greatest sign of respect a dragon could give to any.

He is wasted as an ambassador, to the elves or otherwise, she remarked, her sharp eyes catching the twin scimitars on Galanör's hips. *The world needs rangers like him.*

"Where is Aenwyn?" Asher asked, silently agreeing with his companion's opinion.

"The ports," Galanör informed him, looking out on the crescent, where towers of masts and white sails stood tall. "She's trying to..." The elf trailed off. "It's a long story—older than either of us. But that's why you're here, I assume, to take your place in the *end* of the story? Vighon and Inara said they would seek you out for the job."

Asher chuckled softly to himself. "How many stories have we ended, I wonder," he mused aloud, looking up at Avandriell.

None so old as this one, I think.

"Come then," Galanör bade. "Aenwyn will know to find us in the archives."

Avandriell turned, curling her tail with care to avoid damaging the surrounding buildings. Her wings flared, shading them from the afternoon sun and lending a golden hue to the fleshy membranes. The horses were disturbed all the more by the powerful gust of wind that came off those wings, the dragon launched into the sky at breakneck speed.

Avandriell soared thereafter, a celestial gem of bronze ascending into the heavens on enviable wings. The ranger couldn't help but smile seeing the awe plastered across his friend's face. Any dragon was a sight to behold, but Avandriell was special, a creature of ancient and royal stock.

Again, Galanör had his horse by the reins, one hand caressing the side of its face while he muttered soothingly into one ear. "This is Nölkir," he named lovingly, "a mandräs from The Elmer Forest in Ayda. A gift from Faylen before she departed with the Galfreys."

Asher reached out, his fingers tracing the white line that ran down between the animal's eyes. "A fine gift," he said, thinking of Faylen, her raven hair cascading over her shoulders. He missed her more than he cared to admit.

Walking beside the elf, who towed his mandräs by the reins, they followed the coastal road in the company of those same knights who had escorted Galanör. They had been sent from Valgala, by his accounting, on the orders of Queen Gwenyfer. Their mandate was simple: grant Galanör and any sent by the throne of Illian her authority in all matters pertaining to the Leviathan.

"How have you come to be so far from home?" Asher asked, doing his best to ignore the onslaught of peering eyes and whispered comments. It took him a few streets to realise that the looks and comments were aimed at Galanör and not himself.

Of course, Avandriell said into his mind. *You're just a man in their eyes. They have never seen an elf before. Atilan made their kind in Illian, did he not? They would be among the oldest fables to these people.*

"I thought you and Aenwyn were ambassadors on behalf of the elves," Asher continued. "Ayda's a world away."

Galanör smiled in his disarming way. "You know the hearts of Reyna and Nathaniel better than most. They only want what's best for Verda, and that includes the world of man. If that means releasing their ambassadors to tend a matter between Illian and Erador…"

Asher, indeed, knew well the hearts of two of his oldest and closest friends. The Galfreys would do anything to make the world a better, safer place. They had nearly died several times over doing just that.

Half way down the curved shore, Asher was taken across the lengthy bridge and onto the lone island. The palace, as it were, towered over them soon enough, its grand gates opened wide by the guards who barred the way. Rounding the small garden, the ranger waited while a servant boy accepted the reins from Galanör. His gaze roamed over the ivy that grew up the white walls, carrying his attention across balconies and arching windows. It was certainly more inviting than The Dragon Keep.

"This is home to Blood Lord Thalik and his family," the elf explained, leading the way up the short steps and into the lofty foyer. "They're on their annual pilgrimage to The Red Hold, but they have extended the queen's hospitality and granted us access to the ancient archives."

"The Red Hold?"

Galanör paused, waiting for one of the servants to pass them by. "Erador still clings to its oldest religion. They worship Kaliban here."

There was a name Asher knew well. It was the same religion King Atilan and his wretched ilk had worshipped in their time, ten thousand years ago.

Such worship had lent to the naming of Atilan's secret fortress in the heights of The Vengoran Mountains. It was inevitable that he would then think of Valanis, the dark elf who had found the deep wells of magic Atilan had left in Kaliban. Both he and Galanör had fought Valanis there, in the company of others who would go on to be considered heroes.

The memory of death lingered thereafter, his first life having come to an end in the cold heart of Kaliban.

"The Red Hold is home to The Gilded," Galanör went on, "the priests of Kaliban. It's considered a holy place. The Blood Lord and his family will likely be there until the spring."

The knights left behind, elf and man made their way through the halls until they arrived at an unassuming stairwell in the palace's back corner. It spiralled into the depths of the island, illuminated by regular torches.

"These are the archives of Elderhall," Galanör declared at the bottom, when they were presented with a dozen rows of bookshelves and a single table that ran the length of the chamber. "There is a more extensive athenaeum in the city proper, but the repository there has nothing so old as the vellums down here."

From the look of the long table, where a great number of scrolls, tomes, and parchments lay amidst a plethora of notes, Galanör and Aenwyn had taken to their task with zeal.

Asher picked up a candle in its holder and brought it closer to the notes. "I thought there wasn't much documented on the Leviathan."

"There's a comprehensive list of all the ships and the crews who have set sail and never returned," the elf told him, gesturing to one of the thicker books. "Of the beast itself…" He picked up a quill and waved it over the various parchments and scrolls. "Heresy, conjecture, rumours. There's a lot of myth and legend, and it's all shaded by the distinct note of religion. Finding the real truths has been like navigating a maze."

Asher moved some of the vellum about, scrutinising the very different sketches of the Leviathan. "Any eye-witness accounts? Survivors?"

"Few and far between," the elf replied, rifling through a small pile of scrolls. "Aenwyn has been putting together any shared details."

The ranger accepted the parchment and looked over the finest penmanship he had ever seen. He immediately didn't like what he read. "Boiling water?"

Galanör nodded along. "It's the *one* thing they all have in common. The sea literally boils around it. There was even a couple of reports that told of it melting the hull."

Asher read the litany of adjectives that had been used to describe the Leviathan's scale. "It's big then," he surmised miserably.

"Keep going."

The ranger glanced at his elven friend, not sure he wanted to. "What in the hells is this? It's skin peels off?"

Galanör folded his arms, eyes pinched in consideration. "We're not sure what that one means. There's multiple reports of its skin… coming away. Coming *alive*."

For all the monsters and fiends Asher had slain in his time, he couldn't imagine such a thing. "Its skin comes *alive?*"

The elven ambassador shrugged. "There were a few reports that said as much. *Scavs* they called them."

"Scavs?"

"An old slang most likely." Galanör sifted through the accounts until he found the scroll he was looking for. "Here. Read this one."

"*It's back broke the water, curling into the deep,*" Asher read aloud. "*Monsters there were. Monsters of its own flesh. They peeled off the behemoth and made for the ship. Scavs all they were. They ate my friends, my brothers. They could not be stopped. Their hunger was that of the beast itself, bottomless and black.*" Asher let the report fall onto the table top. "This sounds nothing like the one we fought on Dragorn," he said, trying not to dwell on such grim imagery.

Galanör took to one of the chairs, appearing somewhat lost in it all. "I don't think any two Leviathans are the same."

"What about its hunting grounds?" the ranger enquired. "Have there been any cross-overs? The same waters."

The elf shook his head. "It's claimed ships from north to south, sinking some within eye-line of the shore and others in open waters. It hunts wherever the prey is."

Asher examined one of the sketches more closely. It revealed tentacles lined with claws and each as thick as masts. "Wherever the prey is," he echoed absently. "Have there been reports of bringing down smaller vessels? Rowboats and the like?"

Galanör narrowed his eyes, making a quick survey of the table top. "No," he answered, drawing the word out. "That would make sense, I suppose," the elf deduced. "Everything suggests the Leviathan is gargantuan in size: it would require larger prey."

Slowly making his way down the length of the table, Asher let his blue eyes roam over the work amassed by the elves, his mind churning like the very waves that concealed the Leviathan. He was on the hunt now, a fact that altered his state of mind, his very thought patterns. It was amplified all the more by his bond with Avandriell, a natural predator.

"What are you thinking?" Galanör probed.

Asher did his best to embrace Avandriell's approach to the hunt, his mind plucking at threads from his old life, when *people* were his prey. "You don't just wander into your quarry's territory," he replied.

"You stalk them. Observe them. Understand their patterns. Find their vulnerabilities. I can't do any one of those if I can't see it."

"That's why we're going to bait it," came the response, her words carried on a melodic tone.

Asher looked to the base of the spiral stairs and offered a warm smile. "Aenwyn," he named with that same warmth.

"It's good to see you, Asher." The two embraced as friends.

As ever, when the ranger found himself in Aenwyn's company, he regretted not taking the time to better know the elf. She had completed Galanör in a way that made him a better man—so to speak—but she had done so much more to endear herself to Asher and all. Besides her significant part in the battle of Qamnaran, where Alijah and Malliath had enslaved so many dwarves, Aenwyn had gone on to fight valiantly on The Moonlit Plains against hordes of Reavers. More so, she had been atop The Vrost Mountains, fighting side by side with those few who assaulted The Bastion and challenged Alijah.

She was a hero who had done well to stand apart from the long shadow Galanör cast.

On a personal level, Aenwyn also reminded Asher of Faylen, be it in the style of her long dark hair or the shape of her lips. Elves were nothing if not enchanting.

From over her shoulder, Aenwyn removed her bow and placed it flat on the table. Asher's attention lingered on the weapon, its pure black surface sparkling as if the stars were trapped therein. There was a time when his memories were hazy, fogged by a life of violence and any human's inability to recall distant years. Sharp were those edges now, the haze blown away by the incomprehensible power of dragons.

For just a moment, the ranger was standing atop West Fellion. The fortress was brimming with Graycoats, young and old, naive and experienced, as they looked out on a force of five hundred Arakesh.

The assassins had been led by Adellum Bövö, a dark elf and general under Valanis. The elf had aimed that legendary bow—empowered by Valanis himself—at West Fellion and, with a single arrow, decimated the great doors. Asher had been thrown from the ramparts, where he, alone, had held the line against the invasion.

Since then, Reyna Sevari had put the bow to good use, using it time and time again to strike at evil. It had been a gift worthy of Aenwyn's contributions.

"My hope is renewed to see you here," the elf continued, moving past the ranger to affectionately squeeze Galanör's shoulder. "This is to be no easy hunt."

"You've done well to collate what scraps there are," the ranger complimented. "You have an idea for baiting it?"

"Aenwyn had an idea for baiting it almost immediately," Galanör revealed. "While I was gathering all *this* together, Aenwyn was trawling the ports every day, trying to convince one of the captains in the port to… *doom* their ship." His tone told of the futility in such a task.

"As you said," Aenwyn added, "we can't hunt and kill the fiend if we can't even see it. We need to bait it. Unfortunately, the bait has to be *big*."

"I cannot imagine any captain giving up their vessel," Asher remarked.

"And I found none," Aenwyn confirmed. "Which is why we had to dip into royal coffers."

"You've bought a ship?"

"We've *built* one," the elf specified. "There isn't much industry built around ships the size we need. As such, I found the skeleton of one in the eastern docks, half finished. Coin ran dry some years ago and they abandoned the project. It's needed some replacements here and there and required a lot of man power to make it sea fairing, but we don't need it to operate as a proper ship. It's lacking almost everything a crew would require to live on it."

"It's certainly helped to speed up the process," Galanör commented.

Asher was nodding along, wondering just how long the Draqaros had been searching for him.

"When will it be ready?"

"In a few days," Aenwyn informed him. "We had planned to sail along the coast before then," she said vaguely, looking to Galanör.

"Ah yes," the elf intoned. "I'm afraid the matter is more complicated than you've been led to believe."

Asher looked from Aenwyn to Galanör, a weary expression on his face.

"How so?"

Galanör's smile was just as sharp as his exquisite scimitars.

6

THE GAMBIT

The sky looked to have been set ablaze, burned orange from east to west as twilight reigned over the world. As it did, Asher departed Elderhall on a small ship, chartered days earlier by Aenwyn in anticipation of the journey. The crew consisted of no more than three men—the only three brave enough to sail into the heart of The Dawning Isles.

As they drifted away from Elderhall, their path keeping them within half a mile of the shore, Asher looked up at the sky. He couldn't see Avandriell, but he could feel her in the west, the sun guarding her from sight.

"It would be quicker on dragon back," the ranger had pointed out in the archives, the elves having informed him that The Dawning Isles were two days away by sea.

"Those islands are no place for a dragon," Galanör had warned.

By mid-morning, on the second day, the ambassador's cautionary words made sense to Asher.

Made up of five islands, Erador's largest bay was bristling with defences. From barges and anchored ships to cliff walls and sandy beaches, they were all occupied by ballistas of varying sizes. Piles upon piles of bolts rested beside the weapons, their tips razored and barbed.

Dragon-killers.

Here and there, the ranger even spotted catapults. The inhabitants of The Dawning Isles were prepared for war by sea or air apparently. If their paranoia was anything to go by, Asher reasoned, they looked to already be on a war-footing.

Passing between the first two islands required multiple stops, their way barred by other vessels that had gone out of their way to question them. A degree of bartering was required, sometimes with heated negotiation, though the closer they sailed to the smallest island in the middle of the bay, the more coin they were forced to give over.

While there had been evidence of people living on the larger islands, the smallest was that of an ant hill, teeming with life. The port was a mess and sprawling in every direction as it ringed around the shore, reminding Asher of Dragorn before the island city had been destroyed.

Buildings—all makeshift in their design—had been stacked atop each other at warping angles as they climbed up the central mountain. The centre piece, above the highest row of buildings, was a single ship that looked to have run aground centuries earlier, never to be salvaged or returned to the waters.

The streets wound through the island like serpents, shadowed by rope bridges and thick tethers that kept the general infrastructure held together. So much of it was a haze, fogged by rising smoke from hundreds of chimneys.

It was night by the time they found somewhere to dock, on the fringes of the web-like port. The passing from day to night had done naught to quieten the ram-shackled city. If anything, it was louder in Asher's ears.

Standing upon the edge of the small ship, held fast by one of the sheets in his grip, Asher looked out on it all, his eyes narrowed in assessment. It was a lawless place, attracting the worst of humanity— its predators.

These particular predators went by a specific name: *pirates!*

His instincts battled with themselves. The training that had made him the Arakesh he once was demanded that he adapt and move like a ghost, assuming the role of another inhabitant. The dragon that now lived in his heart had other demands, urging him to display his dominance and superiority as was fitting.

While Avandriell was a fighter through and through, she beheld the wisdom of her kin and always shared it with her companion.

Let the elves take the lead, she told him. *They are ambassadors, after all. Personally,* she added, *I think this is a foolish idea and you should just stay on the boat.*

Asher smirked and glanced at the clouds backlit by the glow of the moon, his eternal companion far from sight.

Hearing the creak of old decking, the ranger turned to see Galanör approaching. Cloaked and hooded, his hands rested on the hilts of his scimitars, Swiftling and Stormweaver. In the blink of an eye he could bring their edges to bear, perhaps the finest swordsman in all of Ayda if not Illian too.

"I thought Gideon had seen to all this," Asher voiced, jutting his chin at the island.

"He did," Galanör assured. "There were many more like the men who rule these islands. Each had their own piece of Erador and they held it by the throat. The pirates were the last he and Ilargo dealt with. Unfortunately, unlike those who reigned over the land, the pirates banded together in the face of their assault. They formed an alliance the war lords and blood barons couldn't conceive of.

"On that day, *Dragon's Bane* was born. The bay is too shallow for the Leviathan and the surrounding islands allow them to defend Dragon's Bane. I heard Gideon and Ilargo tried to assault the city—just the once. It nearly killed Ilargo by all accounts. Since then, they've been allowed to exist outside of Queen Gwenyfer's law, but they are to remain in the bay." Galanör sighed. "That's not always the case, I'm afraid. Allisander, Elderhall, and even as far as Sunhold have all reported of pirate activity. As you can see, they're not just pirates either. Their population has grown. The criminal element of Erador has flocked to this wretched place."

Asher spared Dragon's Bane a glance before returning his attention to the elf. "This is folly, Galanör," he said bluntly, benefiting from their many years of friendship. "You won't find what you're looking for in a place like this."

"I fear you are right, old friend," the elf replied sadly. "But we have to try. Dragon's Bane has the largest—the *only*—fleet in Erador. If we're to battle the Leviathan we need to be out there, on the water, and, preferably, armed to the teeth. Loathsome though they are—and I would spill blood for what they did to Ilargo—these pirates have what we *need*."

"But do *you* have what *they* need?" Asher countered.

"They have no needs here," Aenwyn announced, emerging from the cramped quarters below. "Only *wants*. Only *desires*. We have been given permission from both thrones to treat with them. Be it territory or coin, I'm sure we can appease them."

"I'm assuming Vighon and Inara shared their dream of a unified realm," Asher began, seeing nods from both. "Neither of them will tolerate the threat of pirates in that future. Allowing them to expand and strengthen now only lends them an advantage in the conflict to come."

"Be that as it may," Galanör agreed, "a unified realm will never be accomplished without safe travel across The Hox. We need them if we're going to bury this beast."

Asher clenched his jaw and jumped down onto the deck.

"So be it."

The trio who had crewed the ship thus far bid them luck and gave assurances that they would still be there upon return from their errand. By the look of them and their collective apprehension, the ranger was confident they wouldn't even venture beyond the deck of their ship.

Mimicking his immortal companions, Asher draped his hood, concealing much of his face in shadow as they weaved through the dock. He considered that level of concealment where Galanör and Aenwyn were concerned and was convinced it wouldn't be enough to hide their true nature. Though their pointed ears were the only physical difference at a glance, humans knew, instinctually perhaps, that they weren't looking at another human. They were different. Apart somehow.

Ethereal...

Don't do it, Avandriell warned him. *I know what you're thinking, Ranger. Let them take the lead.*

They're going to stick out.

That might be a good thing considering who you need to speak to. Besides, if you take the lead there's going to be blood.

I can use my words, Asher insisted, doing his best not to sound like a petulant child.

Your words have a tendency to follow your fists. Let the ambassadors do their job.

Asher dipped his head, pushing his sigh right down. **I can say a lot with my fists,** he quipped.

Aenwyn and Galanör paused outside a tavern and exchanged quiet words with the doorman. After a few coins crossed his path, he pointed down the road, directing them to another establishment crammed into the district. The smell of it all fought for dominance, be it the sweat, spices, or meats, both cooked and rancid.

That island and its waters are clear in my eyes, Avandriell told him. *There are more ballistas than I can count. You cannot rely on my interference.*

I don't want you any closer than you already are, Asher was quick to state.

He knew he should have guarded his thoughts the moment he said the words but, it was too late, Avandriell had seen and even felt all that passed through her companion's mind.

You think, the dragon spat, *because Ilargo failed to lay waste to this hive of fiends that I too will succumb to grave injury. You believe Ilargo is stronger than me? Swifter perhaps? Do you also believe that his fire burns hotter than mine?*

Easy, Ava, the ranger bade soothingly, concerned her wrath might descend on the island. *There's no dragon that can beat you at anything. I was thinking only of experience,* he specified. *Ilargo was spearheading assaults and leading armies into battle before you hatched—*

It's not my fault you took so long to be born! Avandriell cut in.

Asher spared the clouded sky a glance while the elves communed with the owner of another tavern. For a price, they were given a new direction, leading them up the winding streets, towards the old ship that had long run aground. It hadn't escaped the ranger that their interactions were being observed by others who lingered nearby, nor that they would take themselves off after hearing who it was the trio had come in search of.

Nearing the top of the rise, Asher lifted his head to better see the ruins of the pirate ship, its hull clinging to the rocks a hundred feet above the highest buildings on the island. Nature had done its best to ensnare the vessel, tangling it in vines and boring through its bowels to sprout new trees.

"This is it," Aenwyn said, her dark eyes roaming over the largest building on the street, a makeshift fort by the look of its high walls.

Lacking the proper materials and architectural input, however, its entrance was no more than a simple door where there should have been grand gates of thick wood or bars of iron. Nor did it occupy any space of its own, the walls plastered to the building next door.

Loud as the streets were, an even more raucous clamour came from inside the fort, a din only found in a crowded bar. There was music too, battling the patrons inside for superiority, which looked to have set off the dogs in the area.

"Hopefully the one we seek is still sober enough to negotiate," Galanör remarked, doubt in his voice.

The elf went on to lead the way, bringing them to that single door in the wall. They had observed a handful of people come and go, the door always operated from the inside after bartering with the eyes that appeared in the narrow slit. It seemed easy enough, despite this being home to Dragon Bane's self-proclaimed king.

Galanör wrapped his knuckles on the wood and waited.

The narrow strip of wood slid aside and those same eyes peered out. "What do you want?" he demanded, voice as ragged as his eyes were bloodshot.

"We have come from Elderhall on behalf of—"

"Piss off!" The eyes vanished and the door was made whole again.

Galanör opened and closed his mouth, taken aback. He knocked again but nobody answered this time. "We might have to rethink our opening strategy," he posed, stepping away from the fort.

Asher frowned, watching the elves fall into quick discussion. "You two have lost your edge," he expressed with a growing smirk on his face.

The ranger reached out and hammered his fist twice into the door. He counted to three in his head and planted himself firmly, feet set apart so his left boot was slightly behind his right.

"Asher!"

Galanör's chastising call came as the eyes appeared again, though his voice was drowned out when the ranger's boot collided with the door.

Wood splintered and hinges snapped as the door was blown in by Asher's boot. So too was the guard launched back, his eyes bruised, nose broken, and lips split.

Without a word to the elves, he stepped inside, entering a quadrangle filled with tables and benches, all packed with patrons, tankards in hand. On the far side there sat a long bar, though much of it was concealed by those trying to buy more drinks.

Every one of them had stopped, their merriment silenced. Their collective gaze was brought down on the shattered entrance, where there now stood a man, hooded and cloaked in green, with a small armoury strapped to his person.

"We're looking for Balthazar Blackhelm!" Asher growled, naming the pirate lord.

As one, the fort's population returned to their conversations, songs, and revelry. The band, nestled in one corner, took up their instruments once more and filled the air with chorale. At his feet, the guard lay flat out beneath the busted door, blood oozing from his nose and mouth.

Galanör appeared at the ranger's side. "I fail to see how this is any better."

"This isn't a place for elven civility," Asher retorted. "And we're *inside*, aren't we?" he added, glimpsing a handful of men peeling away from the inebriated throng.

He had seen men like those all his life, a foul breed that thrived on violence and crowded the dark corners of the world. Untrained brutes who had grown arrogant on the submission of the weak.

"Perhaps these *fine* gentlemen know where we can find Captain Blackhelm," Aenwyn proposed.

Eight there were, and all approaching from different places across the quadrangle. Steel caught in the candlelight, flashing from drawn blades. Asher registered a short scimitar, a pair of daggers, a couple of broadswords, and even a hammer. How were they to know that such weapons would be useless against their intended victims?

The ranger placed a hand on Galanör's forearm, preventing him retrieving his scimitars. "This is all part of the introduction," he informed the elf, before removing his hood. "They're just to be broken, not killed."

"I see," Galanör replied, his eyes darting to the balcony above the bar, where he had spotted the same shadow Asher had noted after the merriment had continued.

They were being observed.

Asher took a calming breath, his nerves and muscles aligning during those precious seconds, the calm before the storm.

The first thug to *introduce* themselves came at the ranger. His knuckles were paled about the hammer's shaft, his crooked teeth gritted together in a manacle smile. The size of his arms suggested he had been wielding that hammer for some time, his muscles having adapted to its weight and balance. His left eye, however, was as pale as fog, the skin above and below scarred from an old injury. It was all the weakness Asher needed.

As was required with any hammer blow, the weapon needed lifting before it could come down, unlike a sword that could be flicked up, thrusted, or slashed. The ranger had only to pivot, repositioning himself to the man's left as the blow fell. His arm already cocked, Asher threw his knotted fist out like a battering ram. The pirate didn't see the attack, and whether he even felt his jaw breaking was questionable as he appeared unconscious before he slammed into the floor.

Only feet away, Galanör was weaving between the broadswords, his hands lashing out one after the other. His left hand caught one in the throat, staggering him in a choking mess, while the other received a knock to the temple, robbing him of all sense. A third came for the elf, his small scimitar hacking inelegantly at the air. Galanör moved like water, as if his body wasn't constrained by the rigidity of a skeleton.

He landed a gut punch so severe it put the thug on his tiptoes. Bent over now, his back was used by the elf to roll over and swing a devastating kick into the side of another's head. Elven strength saw the man fly like a rag doll until he landed on a pair of stools, shattering them into splinters.

Her bow still strapped to her back, Aenwyn moved through the remaining four like a river might cut through a valley. Try as they might, no pirate could touch her. Supernatural were her instincts, as if she knew where the attacks were always coming from, even when she couldn't see her opponent.

One fool came at her with a mighty swing of his axe, as if such a weapon required that much force to cause damage. Using his inexperience against him, Aenwyn seized his arm and rolled her body up and round, feet first, until she was standing on stone once more. In the process, the pirate had been twisted by the point of his now dislocated shoulder, and flipped onto his back, where a swift heel to the face put him into a deep slumber.

The surviving three should have foreseen their inevitable fate, but it seemed the will of their pirate lord drove them on.

Two of them descended on Asher at the same time, bringing daggers and a short-sword to bear against him. As one of the two daggers came for his throat, the ranger batted the arm aside, shoving the man's fist into his comrade's face. That kept the short-sword at bay for a moment longer and allowed Asher to twist the dagger-man around and boot him in the back.

Unfortunately for him, he was forced into Galanör's path. The elf had seen the man coming and leaped at the precise second that would bring his knee up into the thug's face.

The sound of steel slicing through the air reminded Asher that the short-sword was still in play. A simple shift in his shoulders saw the blade cleave through the air only an inch from his arm. The ranger dashed into the man, his fists whipping out in quick succession. Kidneys, solar plexus, jaw—in that order. The short-sword fell from his limp grasp and his body unceremoniously met the ground with a *thud*.

Again, the occupants had grown still, tankards resting on dry lips and eyes wide in shock. There was but a single sound, leading Asher's attention to Aenwyn—specifically, the man she was holding by the throat. He was lifted bodily from the ground, his feet shaking and hands pawing hopelessly at the elf's vice-like grip. His gurgles and sputtering breath echoed across the quadrangle until she released him and the pirate crumpled at her feet.

Asher gave a quiet, if frustrated sigh. "Well there's no hiding what you are now," he muttered, his words caught by sensitive elven ears alone.

One after the other, Galanör and Aenwyn removed their hoods and stood proud before the people of Dragon's Bane. Their immortality was there to see, an aura that could always be sensed by the mortally doomed.

A slow *clap* resonated from the balcony as the shadow stepped into the light. With no shirt on, the light rippled over his muscles, displaying no lack of scars and even a few burns. His face was no exception, his copper goatee run through by a pale gash that tore up through his left cheek. The worst of his burns had ravaged the right side of his head, preventing his hair from growing on that section of scalp.

For all the violence he had clearly endured and the scars that marred his body, Asher's gaze was drawn to that which he wore upon his head. A black crown of knotted and gnarly wood, its exterior littered with short spikes and thorns.

Balthazar Blackhelm.

The pirate lord of Dragon's Bane.

"Welcome! Welcome!" he cheered, a wicked grin twisting his scars. "It's not every day we receive visitors so interesting as yourselves! Won't you come in?"

7

THE PIRATE LORD

Escorted up to the fort's first floor and Balthazar's personal chambers, the trio now stood in a room of opulence not to be found outside those four walls.

Men and women, most in some state of undress, lounged about, always within reach of a pipe or a goblet of dark and potent liquid. They watched the companions as if they were hungry dogs, just waiting for their leader to unleash them.

Between them all, the chamber was decorated with gold and silver trappings, including the frames that contained grand portraits and landscapes of Erador. It felt so incongruous with the stuffed animal heads that had been mounted here and there—especially the enormous hog that stared at the ranger with dead eyes.

Walking over the expensive rugs that lay haphazardly about the floor, Asher came to stand before the throne of Dragon's Bane. It was all too ostentatious for the likes of a pirate lord, its cushioned bottom and arms too plush in their royal purple, and the gilding too extravagant. Here was a man who fancied himself a king, but was condemned to lord over naught but scraps.

Asher knew, there and then, that man could never be negotiated with.

"You sought me out by name," the pirate lord began, sitting lazily on his throne. "You have me at a disadvantage."

His chestnut hair draped over his chest, Galanör bowed his head curtly. "I am Galanör of House Reveeri. This is Aenwyn of House Kirion. We are elves, hailing from the land of Ayda, two oceans away from here."

"Elves…"

The name looked to have been drawn from Balthazar's lips by pure wonderment. And a hungry note of greed, Asher detected.

Galanör ploughed on, unperturbed. "We are ambassadors of Queen Reyna and King Nathaniel Galfrey. We work on behalf of the elven people to help better the world of man wherever we can—wherever we are needed. Thanks to the grace of your queen, Gwenyfer of the Blood Valayan, our aid and wisdom has been extended beyond Illian, to the fair shores of Erador."

Balthazar made a point to look about his chamber. "I see no queen here. The Blood Valayan does not hold sway over this island nor any in the bay." Galanör made to reply but the pirate lord cut him off with a blunt question. "And who are you?" he asked of the ranger, one eye cocked. "You're certainly no elf."

You have no idea what I am, Asher thought.

Galanör pivoted to regard the ranger. "This is… *Asher*."

"That's *it*? Just… *Asher*?"

"I've never needed any more," the ranger replied gruffly.

Balthazar cocked his head, eyes narrowed. "That accent… I'm not familiar with it. Another man spoke to me once, many years ago, with an accent I couldn't place. His name was *Gideon Thorn*. Perhaps you've heard of him since—I assume—you hail from Illian as well."

"I know Thorn," Asher responded, his expression so stoic as to give naught else away.

The pirate lord looked to the pauldron on Asher's right shoulder and jutted his chin. "The Dragon Rider sported similar armour," he observed, suspicion in his tone. "Not bronze like yours, but scales of beautiful green, like his wretched dragon, *Ilargo*." Balthazar spat on the floor, a sneer creasing his face. "So tell me, *east-born*, have you come, as Gideon Thorn did, to try and take what is mine?"

"Our quarrel is not with you, Captain Blackhelm," Galanör assured.

"*King* Blackhelm," the pirate intoned, gesturing to the crown on his head. "I'm not wearing this for amusement." His eyes flashed over Asher, who didn't hide his judgement on the matter. "You think I cannot call myself as much," he deduced.

Asher didn't blink. "I think having a big chair and a piece of driftwood on your head doesn't make anyone a king."

It was subtle, his head slightly bowed, but Galanör winced at the biting words.

Balthazar squared himself before the ranger. "Tell me of a king that didn't take his throne by the blood in his veins or the blood on his hands. After hundreds of years, kings and queens grow fat and lazy on their thrones but, if you go back far enough, they're killers *all*. Murderers and conquerors who took what they wanted and dared any to challenge them."

An awkward and tense silence clung to the air between the men, broken only when Galanör cleared his throat.

"We have not come to dispute title nor land, *King* Blackhelm. If anything, our presence here will only benefit you."

"Your words are like honey, elf, but they are still just *words*. How *exactly* am I to benefit? I see no gifts, no chests overflowing with coins. Unless," Balthazar posed, his voice adopting a seductive tone. "Unless *you* are my gifts." His gaze roamed ravenously over the pair. "I never thought to have an elf for a pet, let alone *two*," he said to himself. "Is it true what they say? That you never age, your bodies and minds trapped just as they are... *forever*."

The immortals shared a brief, if uncomfortable, glance.

"We did not travel thousands of miles and risk death in the north to present ourselves as *gifts*," Aenwyn stated firmly. "And what we have to offer must first be *earned*."

A devilish smile slowly carved its way through Balthazar's face. "So it's true then: you have come to slay the Leviathan!" Laughter broke out of his mouth and the chamber's occupants accompanied him, filling the room with their vile amusement. "My little birdies hear everything," he boasted, wagging a finger at the elves. "Your dummy ship nears completion, aye? Are you hoping the beast will choke on it?" Again, the sycophants that surrounded the pirate lord mimicked his insulting mirth.

"If you know our intentions," Galanör said, cutting through the laughter, "then are we to assume you know why we're here?"

"No such word has reached my ears," Balthazar admitted, his amusement slow to burn away. "But I can guess!"

The pirate lord jumped to his feet and moved towards the balcony that overlooked the quadrangle and all of Dragon's Bane.

"The good Queen Gwenyfer," he began, and mockingly so, "might have extended you her authority on the mainland, but she has no such *navy* to extend to you." He turned to face the trio, a smug grin revealing stained teeth. "You can't kill the sea beast from the shore. You need ships. *Lots* of ships. Ballistas too I'd wager. Like those," he added with a wink, the distant masts and sails catching in the moonlight.

"Slaying the Leviathan benefits *everyone*," Aenwyn insisted. "How long have you and your ancestors been chained to the shallows? There's a whole world out there. Imagine the seas with open waters from east to west."

Balthazar wandered along their line. "I *imagine* the lives and resources Queen Gwenyfer will spend trying to beat such a foe. In that world, her shiny new realm will be in so much debt, the throne will come running to *me* for a loan. Can *you* imagine the leverage I'll have then? The Blood Valayan will be no more than a puppet on a paper throne."

"There's no guarantee on that outcome," Galanör pointed out.

The pirate lord stopped in front of Aenwyn and spun on his heel to face the other elf.

"And is that what you bring me, Galanör of House Reveeri? Guarantees? The last man who came here with guarantees could not deliver on his word, but he did leave a *mark*."

Asher was drawn to the old burns on the side of Blackhelm's head, though he couldn't decide whether they had been caused by dragon fire or Gideon's magic.

Galanör raised his chin a notch, not one to be intimidated.

"Guarantees are exactly what we bring, and with sealed approval, no less, from the thrones of Illian *and* Erador." At that, the elf removed a folded and ribboned bundle of parchments from within his cloak.

Balthazar accepted the vellum, if hesitantly, but he did not move to read what lay inside. "I would hear more of those honeyed words," he said instead, looking deliberately to Aenwyn. "Tell me: what will I find in here exactly?"

For just a moment, Aenwyn's features became all the more defined as she tensed her jaw.

"In the case of the Leviathan's removal," she began, "trade routes will be established between Illian and Erador. A whole new industry of imports and exports will be birthed upon the waters of The Hox, a most *lucrative* industry. For any with the resources to take part, it would be the opportunity of a lifetime.

"Of course," she continued, "this would prove troublesome for those of Dragon's Bane, as any and all are considered to be pirates and are therefore subject to the laws of *both* realms. The papers you hold in your hand, King Blackhelm, detail your pardon should you prove an ally in the hunt and extermination of the Leviathan."

Balthazar's eyebrows rose at that. "A pardon?"

"You said it yourself," Galanör reminded. "Queen Gwenyfer has no such navy. *You* have the ships. You could play a vital role establishing the new trade routes. You could build an empire inside the confines of the law and enjoy a different kind of freedom."

"See me as a merchant, aye? A man of business and contracts—a tax paying citizen who spends his days sat behind a desk looking over stock lists and crew manifests." He sniggered at that before growing serious. "And what of my kingdom? My crown? What happens to Dragon's Bane in this new world?"

Aenwyn paused, her concern for where the negotiation was going all too evident. "You may take any title you wish should it pertain to the work of establishing the trade routes and ports. I'm afraid there's just no room for another crown. In either realm."

Balthazar was too calm given what he stood to lose. He wandered back to his throne, nodding along, appearing to be in deep thought. Seated once more, he produced a slender knife from his belt and held it lazily, so the point stabbed into one of the armrests, where he could twiddle it endlessly.

"No," he said simply.

Galanör blinked. "No?"

"No," the pirate lord repeated. "I do not accept these terms. Queen Gwenyfer had others fight for her crown. I *bled* for mine," he said through gritted teeth. "Neither she nor any foreign king or queen can take that from me. My claim to this bay and these waters will not be brought into question by the acceptance of any *pardon*.

"However!" he exclaimed, his mood shifting from anger to intrigue. "I do see great potential in this *new world*. You're quite right; safe passage from shore to shore will prove most lucrative. The coins will flow from east *and* west. The only real question is: who will *grant* such passage?"

Galanör was too old and too wise to misunderstand the man. "You would rule The Hox and control the trade routes."

Balthazar beamed. "I accept!" he cried dramatically.

"Those are not the terms we offer," Aenwyn stated firmly.

"No," the would-be king agreed, "but they are the terms your kings and queens will have to live with."

"There's still the matter of the Leviathan," Asher reminded.

"Then take heart!" Balthazar urged. "You came seeking my help in slaying the monster and that's exactly what I'll do! I will bring the might of Dragon's Bane down on the fiend, a fleet unlike any the creature has ever seen. Then," he proclaimed, standing now with one foot resting on his throne, "upon my triumphant victory, I will expand my kingdom to every corner of The Hox. Every man, woman, and child under my rule will sleep on a bed of coins," he told them smugly.

His cold eyes fell on the trio. "You have my gratitude for bringing this to my attention. I look forward to conveying my intentions to Queen Gwenyfer in person, after she's thanked me, of course."

"I'm confident no such meeting shall take place," Galanör replied curtly. "Your intentions, however, will be relayed to the relevant sovereigns. Good evening."

The elf turned to leave and found a wall of pirates and thugs had moved to bar the way.

"We came as *messengers*," he pointed out, looking back at King Blackhelm.

"Messengers?" Balthazar echoed in disbelief. "Do not trip over your own words, elf. You came here to take my throne and my crown, as if your offer was anything but a vow to conquer Dragon's Bane. Worse: I was to be pleased that the *girl* would pardon me for doing the same thing her ancestors did and taking what I could. Unlike her, I do not hide what I am. I take what I can, *because* I can. No," he said, shaking his head. "You did not come here as messengers. You came as *heralds of doom*. I will not quaver."

Galanör faced the king now, his blue cloak draped back just enough to grant quick and easy access to his scimitars. "We *are* leaving this island."

"I don't see how," the pirate lord uttered, the threat of Galanör's wrath lost on him. "The crew who brought you here have already been fed to the pigs."

Get out, Avandriell snapped.

Asher could feel her drawing closer. **Stay away**, he cautioned.

"You dare!" Galanör raged, his hands gripped to his hilts now.

"You are three against thousands," Balthazar remarked casually, "and with no way off this island. Submit to me peacefully, and he will be granted a quick death," he promised, gesturing at Asher. "Draw steel and we'll break every bone in his body before throwing him in with the pigs."

Run! Avandriell implored.

The ranger turned his mouth to the elves, his eyes never straying from Blackhelm.

"*The balcony,*" he said in their fair tongue, bringing out a frown in Balthazar.

"*We won't make it to the shore,*" Galanör replied, his words lost on the pirate lord.

Asher paused, his lips having just parted, when he glimpsed into Avandriell's mind and gleaned her intentions. "*Now!*" he demanded in elvish.

As one, the trio darted to the left and dashed across the balcony with every pirate in pursuit. In synchronicity, they flew over the rail and landed amidst the many patrons in a jump that would have broken bones in any other. Disgruntled by the dramatic interruption, the people of Dragon's Bane hollered at the companions, who fled on light and quick feet towards the fort's only door.

Balthazar Blackhelm shoved his men aside and pressed himself into the railing, his voice booming over the din. "Grod!"

The ground shook three times. It was all the warning they received before the wall beside the door was blown in, the stone split apart and shattered to make way for something so big it couldn't fit through the door.

Asher had shielded his eyes from the debris, missing the point at which the fort had accepted a new patron.

His gaze steadily rose, taking in the slabs of muscle and grubby appearance of a man so tall and wide it was an impossibility he was a man at all. That's because he wasn't, the ranger knew, his memory pulling not from Avandriell but from Thessaleia, her mother.

He stood in the shadow of a Giant of The Glimmer Lands.

8

THE ⊙F MY ENEMY

Asher had seen the Giant's ilk before, when his bond with Avandriell was still young and raw, and her mother's memories were all she clung to.

Thessaleia had stood watch, all those millennia ago, while her Rider conversed with a group of the behemoths. As the ranger had noted in the memory then, he saw with his own eyes now that the creature was nothing like the Giants who roamed the wilds of Illian.

Grod, as his master had named him, stood three times Asher's height, but that still placed him at half the size of a Giant native to the east. His features, while larger in every way, were notably human in structure, if well hidden behind a matted mane of wild hair and a beard so thick it concealed his neck. Still, it wasn't enough to hide the tough leather collar or the chains that hung limp from his fastenings. He was a slave.

Before the dust could settle about the Giant, Grod dipped his head and unleashed a snarling growl. It would have been all the more terrible had it not been drowned out by a thunderous roar, a sound so terrifying it silenced all of Dragon's Bane.

The fort's inhabitants, including Grod the Giant, ignored the escaping trio and turned their gaze on the dark mountain slope. There they found a hulking shadow, a Wraith of destruction, moving beyond the shipwreck.

All at once there came the sound of splintering wood, snapping trees, and the churning of earth amidst crumbling stone.

It took everyone a moment longer than it should have to see the truth of the calamity.

Then came the screams and cries of dread, including a gasp from Grod, who turned and charged back through the jagged hole he had created. Asher was close on the Giant's heels and the elves on his.

As they passed behind the walls, the ranger dared to look back. He saw Balthazar Blackhelm scrambling over the railing and taking his chances with the drop.

Further up the slope, doom was descending on Dragon's Bane at speed, the old ship tumbling and buckling under its own weight. Dragging long ropes in its wake, the mast snapped free and hurtled towards the fort like a battering ram. It was accompanied by an army of debris, the ship's total tonnage reduced to an avalanche of wood and iron.

The cascade brought about an almighty crash that swept through the fort and the buildings on either side. The mast shot through it all and continued down to the next level of Dragon's Bane.

It took Grod with it, the broken end slamming into the Giant at speed.

Asher jumped as far down the street as he could, hoping to avoid the bulk of the debris. The impact was tenfold given that it decimated the fort and added every inch of it to the cascading storm.

Something heavy struck the ranger in the shoulder, flinging him from his feet and launching him through a door on the other side of the street. Only a heartbeat later and the opposing wall was ripped away. Fearing collapse, Asher pushed himself up and dived through the window, avoiding the weight of the building before it folded on itself.

Choking on thick dust, his vision hampered, he didn't fight the strong hand that gripped him by the arm and dragged him down the street. He stumbled here and there, his feet catching chunks of debris or strewn bodies.

On the edge of the impact site now, the ranger blinked hard and rubbed his eyes to see Galanör and Aenwyn, both coated in dust. He nodded his thanks and turned back. The ship had gone on to create chaos on the next level down, felling trees and buildings alike.

Ava, did you just drop a **ship** *on me?*

Yes, and you're squandering the opportunity! Get to the north side, now.

The north side?

Their ballistas are fewer and there's space for me to land on the shore. Go!

From the looming mountain, billowing wings buffeted the night air. Avandriell remained a shadow up there, her path carefully chosen to avoid the moonlight.

Through the growing haze in front of them, figures began to take shape. Survivors. The lucky few who had brushed with Death and lived to tell of it. They staggered through the mess of it all, bleeding from various wounds, their eyes wide in astonishment—in shock. One such figure had a familiar face; a thug from Balthazar's throne room. His sight narrowed on them, his confusion turning to rage.

"You!" he bellowed, before tripping over a body.

"We need to get out of here," Aenwyn insisted.

"Ava will meet us on the north side," Asher reported, turning to run by their side.

"No!" Galanör protested, shoving his way through the onlookers who had appeared. "They'll shoot her down, Asher."

"Honestly," the ranger replied, guiding them down an alley to the lower level, "I wouldn't argue with her."

Somewhere in the darkness of night, there came a shattering roar that tore the air asunder—someone out there *was* arguing with the dragon.

After descending another tier, doing their best to cut through where they could and avoid the winding road, they began to hear the distinct sound of ballista bolts whistling through the air to the north. It was soon followed by the sound of destruction and even a distant explosion. While the view to the north was obstructed by buildings, an orange aura tinted the night's sky over the rooftops as dragon fire graced the shoreline.

Galanör stopped, his arms stretched out to prevent Asher and Aenwyn from going any further down the street. His keen senses had saved them all, and by no more than a single step.

All three of their cloaks were swept out in the wake of the broken mast, the length of wood shoved across the muddy ground at neck-breaking speed. The ranger hardly saw it, a dark blur that went on to obliterate a tanner's shop and bring the rest of the building down on top of it.

Turning from the plume of dust and debris, Asher laid eyes on the one who had launched the broken mast. So too did those who had been running through the street with buckets of water. They scattered to the alleys, seeking a different route to the numerous fires that now threatened Dragon's Bane.

None wished to come between the Giant and his foes.

Marred by a thousand cuts, including a nasty gash that had robbed the fiend of his left eye, Grod clenched his fists into enormous knots of bone and muscle before bellowing into the night. It was a promise of vengeance.

Asher gripped the hilt of his broadsword, his mind slipping into that familiar space where he shared all with Avandriell. It was always jarring when the dragon was in the throes of violence, her thoughts lowered to a more animalistic and predatory state of mind. It was all fire and ripping and crunching, his senses almost overloaded by the smell and taste of ash, blood, and sweat.

Ava, I need your mother's memories now, he intoned.

Grod charged at the trio, his every footfall shaking the earth beneath their boots. Like wheat in a field, the companions dispersed around the Giant, each flexing and bending as required to see them to safety. The hulking beast charged into the debris with naught but air caught between his thick arms.

Galanör sprang from his dive and roll with Stormweaver in one hand and Swiftling in the other. Aenwyn, light of foot, had run up and along the wall of a butcher's shop, taking her clear over the Giant.

Asher lacked their inherent grace and agility, but his bond with Avandriell enhanced his every ability, and so the ranger was able to rise smoothly from his leaping corkscrew.

The air was cleaved by the high toned ring of silvyr, his broadsword freed from its scabbard.

Ava? he growled, his knees crouched and ready to spring.

I'm a little busy, mud-walker! came her terse response.

Thessaleia knew their language, Asher said, putting some distance between him and the elves as Grod picked himself up.

You don't need words to cut that thing's head off! Just use the pointy end!

He's not like our Giants! Search your mother's memories. They're like us—me—just… bigger. He doesn't have to die.

It would certainly be quicker!

Asher got the strong impression that Avandriell was running out of time. *Just give me the language!* he fumed, skidding on his knees to avoid a swinging arm and snatching fingers.

There sounded a tornado in the north as the dragon spat forth another jet of fire along the coast.

Brace yourself, she warned.

The ranger staggered to his left, his mind having sprung a leak. For just a moment, he forgot the very shape of words, his tongue and lips numb to the many languages he had learned.

Fortunately, Grod had targeted the elusive elves, who darted in and out of his attacks like flies. Frustrated, the Giant grasped a chain in each hand and yanked both with all his strength. Taut in his grip, his veins bulged as he tried to separate them from his collar.

It was all the time Galanör needed to race past and run his fine blades through Giant flesh. Swiftling scored a red line across his ribs before its companion, Stormweaver, gouged a bloody tear across his hip. Grod roared in pain, but the agony of his wounds lent him the strength he needed, and the chains came free. His technique was undoubtedly clumsy, but in his hands they were still deadly whips.

Aenwyn cartwheeled to her right, her body moving in time with the lashing chain. The metal *cracked* against the ground and the air whistled as the second chain chased after her. The elf ran straight up the nearest wall and flipped backwards, narrowly evading the *whip-crack* of the second chain by a hair's breadth.

Galanör brought his own weapons to bear and cut through the iron links as they came for him. He held Stormweaver aloft and allowed one of the chains to coil about the blade. When the chain was taut, Swiftling sliced from high to low, shortening it beyond use.

Faster than his size would have suggested, Grod snatched at the elf and gripped him by the chest in a single hand. The Giant bled for it, his forearm split open by two scimitars, but he still tossed Galanör liked a rage doll into the nearest wall.

"*Stop!*" Asher yelled, the sound of the word foreign even to his own ears.

Grod's massive head swivelled on the ranger, his solid brow creasing into a frown.

"*We're not your brother,*" the ranger said desperately, one hand held flat out to the Giant. He quickly realised the wrong word had left his lips. "*Enemy,*" he spat. "*We're not your enemy. We... friends!*" Asher beat his chest and gestured at the elves. "*Boat... erm.*" He stumbled over the words as they poured out of Avandriell's deep memory. "*Boat-people—bad,*" he said, unable to find a word to accurately describe a *pirate*. "*Help. Friends. Follow. Get off... rock.*"

Grod stood a little straighter, his good eye fixed on the ranger. "*How does a little one come to know such a tongue?*" His voice was so deep it almost robbed his words of definition.

"Asher?" Galanör's warning tone led the ranger to a cluster of figures running towards them from up the hill.

Ignoring both the elf and the approaching fight for the moment, Asher kept his attention on Grod.

"Need to get out of there... here. Have to swim—run. Have to run. North," he specified, pointing. *"Follow. No chains,"* he added, mimicking a collar about his neck.

"Asher." Galanör's tone had adopted an even more serious tone, his scimitars flicking up into a ready position.

"Are we running or fighting?" Aenwyn asked, retrieving Adellum's bow from over her shoulder.

"That's up to him," Asher uttered, searching the Giant's only eye for any hint of his intentions.

Believing Grod still fought for their pirate lord, the thugs charged without thought—swords, axes, and hammers raised. Their beliefs were misplaced.

The Giant swept one hand out and round. The first to meet his knuckles died instantly, his neck snapped. The second was knocked unconscious when the first man slammed into him, but Grod's fist went on to club a third, launching him through someone's front door and out of sight.

The remaining men faced a critical decision in that moment. Three of them chose life and peeled away at speed, vanishing down the closest alleyway. Confronted by a wall of muscle and rage, the other four were either frozen with fear or too stupid to realise they were no match for a Giant.

Grod stepped forwards and clapped his hands together. Unfortunately for two of Balthazar's men, they were standing side by side inside those closing palms.

The sound of roaring fires and constant yelling masked the sound of their skulls smashing into one, but there was nothing to mask the sight of so much blood squirting between Grod's fingers. Foolishly, the other two missed their opportunity to flee and, instead, jabbed their swords at the Giant's back. He cried out in pain, turning on the thugs with gritted teeth.

Asher could only watch the unbridled strength of the Giant, his hands encompassing a head each. The men's screams of terror and pain were muffled by thick palms, but they didn't suffer for long. *"Boat men—bad!"* he yelled, clenching his fists.

His hands slick with blood, bone fragments, and brain matter, the Giant turned to the ranger. *"Friends,"* he declared.

The ranger gave a simple nod and looked to his elven companions. "He's with us. Let's go."

It was somewhere between horror and disgust that both Galanör and Aenwyn observed the Giant's bloody work. "You're sure?" the archer asked.

He wasn't sure at all, but they were running out of time—Avandriell had informed him of ships converging on her location. "Let's go!" he replied instead.

With Grod at their back, they experienced no further delays on their way down the island. Running parallel to the sprawling port, they continued up the shore and into the north, where Dragon's Bane tailed off and the harbour thinned.

Asher's first glimpse of Avandriell was in the light of her own fire, her bat-like wings fanned out as she towered over a barge lined with ballistas. Some of the pirates manning it dove over the edge and took their chances in the dark waters. Those who remained were torched in a single breath.

Her wings fanned the flames as she took off once more, avoiding bolts flying in from open waters, where new ships were arriving. The ranger was dismayed to see the numerous holes that punctured Avandriell's membranes. He could also feel—absent any pain—the quartet of ballista bolts that protruded from her back left leg and a lone bolt that had impacted the right side of her tail.

She was furious. The emotion burned bright in her, threatening to bleed into Asher. Somewhat worried that the dragon would fall into a frenzy that would blind her to their peril, the ranger updated her on their location and their new... ally.

Flying low, wing tips and tail skimming the bay's surface, Avandriell weaved between the ships. Try as they might, the pirates were too slow to get the ballistas reorganised and their aims lined up. One swing of her tail capsized one of the smaller ships before her right wing tore through the mast and rigging of another.

Grod came to a sudden halt on the glassy beach, his huge and bare feet crunching through the super-heated sand. "*No*," he proclaimed, eyes wide as he took in the wrath of Avandriell. "*Fire Snake!*" At once, the Giant changed direction and ran for his life.

"*Fire Snake is friend!*" Asher called after him, but it was no use—his strides put him beyond pursuit.

"Look!"

Galanör was pointing at a plateau a hundred feet up the side of the mountain, where even more ballistas sat waiting to be manned. Indeed, they soon would be. A dozen men were running up the path, each hoping they would be the one to bring down the dragon.

Asher pivoted to look out on the sea.

Ava, we're here!

The bronze dragon roared, pained by another ballista, its bolt having caught her front right shoulder.

"Avandriell!" the ranger blared aloud.

Without warning, she dipped her head and plunged into the water, wings folded in. Waves were sent in every direction, rocking the smaller ships and anchored barges. Without warning, two of the latter were dragged from their place in the water until they collided with each other, sending every man from both into the sea's cold embrace.

All went quiet after that, save a handful of bolts that were fired into the depths. There came a constant call for reload, the war machines in constant need of new bolts.

"Get ready," Asher warned, sheathing his sword.

Galanör and Aenwyn mirrored his action and replaced their weapons. They had no idea what was coming. Neither did anyone else, which is why it came as such a terrifying event when, at last, Avandriell launched out of the sea like a demon born of its black depths, her wings unfurled.

Her front claws gripped to the hull of a medium-sized vessel and dug deep as she rose ever higher. The crew screamed as the deck beneath their feet shifted dramatically, throwing all of them from port to starboard. They each plunged into the waters and were soon followed by their ship as it rolled over and onto its side.

A hail of bolts split the air, a couple of which pierced Avandriell's wings and skimmed the bony joint. Her retribution was Death made manifest. The dragon opened her mouth and banished the night. In the light of her flames, the devastation was clear to see, including the men who ran for their lives. None made it to the water before her fire engulfed them.

Gliding low and round from the northern waters, Avandriell made for the beach. She had only to turn her head and exhale to make a ruin of the ballistas built into the mountainside. Those that had taken aim at her were just as blackened and charred as the wood they had operated.

Sweeping over the beach now, her speed was enough to extinguish the smaller fires that still licked at the air.

Asher was already running in the same direction and the elves with him. Only those with the abilities of a Rider or an elf could hope to pull off such a manoeuvre, and so they used their enhancements to their advantage.

One after the other, and all in the blink of an eye, they reached out and gripped one of the bony protrusions that grew out of Avandriell's tail. Asher felt the extreme pressure exerted against his shoulder, where his arm threatened to lose its place in the joint.

Ultimately, the dragon's speed took the trio from their feet as she raced across the shore. Upon her companion's request, and reluctantly so, her left claw extended to ensnare Grod, who had not stopped in his effort to reach the southern coast and get as far away from the Fire Snake as possible.

The Giant cried out in protest, his considerable bulk no more than a pebble in Avandriell's grip. He ceased his flailing when the dragon flapped her wings and banked around the south side of the island, weaving and dodging between the bolts that splintered the air. For the time being, it was all Asher and the elves could do to stay secured against her tail.

That became harder after she curled round the shore and left the port behind. Her horned head lifted to the sky, her body following, taking all of them into a vertical lift up the side of the island's prominent mountain.

The open sky was a welcome sight, where the ballistas could no longer chase them. Dipping her right wing, Avandriell turned around and flew into the west, making, once again, for Elderhall.

She had left Dragon's Bane on fire.

9

THE INDEBTED

"Stop squirming," Asher snapped, his feet pressed against Avandriell's back left leg, his body almost horizontal.

In his white-knuckled grip was the last of the four ballista bolts that had pierced her side. The ranger pushed in with his feet and pulled hard with his hands. He was forced to twist the haft to loosen it, eliciting a roar from the dragon.

It made the Giant wince, who had been sure to keep some distance between him and Avandriell since they had landed late that morning.

Get on with it! Avandriell growled across their bond.

"Almost... got it."

At last, the final bolt was jarred free of its lodging, taking Asher to the grassy knoll on which they had settled. The ranger picked himself up and tossed the bolt on the pile he had formed, including the bolt that had been embedded in her tail.

"Just one left," he said, thinking of the bolt stuck in her front right shoulder.

The dragon snarled and whipped her head around to the right. Asher couldn't see, but he heard the bolt be tugged free by powerful jaws. Avandriell turned to see him before spitting the bolt on the ground and exhaling sharply through her nostrils.

Asher knew her well enough to know the dragon was using her anger to conceal pain. He rubbed her injured leg, noting the dark stain of blood upon the bronze scales. She was lucky the pirates didn't have access to silvyr. Had their bolts been tipped with such, they would have gone through and through, causing catastrophic damage.

You should have stayed out of it, he said dismissively, annoyed that she had put herself in that kind of danger.

Do not mistake me for some beast of burden, Ranger. I go where I please.

It's luck one of those bolts didn't find your heart.

Luck! the dragon echoed venomously. *You would rob me of skill and have me thank dumb luck for saving you all from death?*

I would have you think twice before risking your life to save me! Don't throw away immortality just because you think I might die! I've survived more than most, Ava. Next time, just wait.

Avandriell shifted her position so she could bring her face that much closer to his.

You haven't always survived, she reminded him. *And I would burn the world and face the wrath of the sun itself to save you. Just as you would…*

With that, her ragged wings beat the air, blowing the grass out in every direction. Asher raised his gaze with her ascension, his hair and cloak whipped out behind him. She was already following her nose, her acute senses having detected potential prey on the breeze.

"Was that as tense as it looked?" Galanör enquired, crouched effortlessly atop the only boulder in the field.

Asher sighed, feeling his bond with Avandriell diminish with every second.

"We've agreed to disagree," he said simply, his eyes falling on Swiftling, the scimitar gleaming in the elf's hand. "You don't need that," the ranger told him, glancing at Grod in the distance—the Giant was watching Avandriell closely. "He was a prisoner on that island. We just freed him."

Galanör didn't look convinced. "He's a Giant, Asher. They don't think like we do."

"You've never encountered his kind before," the ranger replied. "They're different."

"I saw what he did to those men. That didn't look different to me."

"You spoke to him," Aenwyn commented, her purple cloak billowing about her. There was also something of a question in her tone.

"Avandriell's mother—Thessaleia—knew their language; her Rider had dealings with them. Thankfully, their tongue hasn't changed much in the millennia since."

One of Aenwyn's immaculate eyebrows raised a notch. "You can access languages through your bond?" she asked with wonder. "I've never heard of that."

Asher wouldn't recommend it to other Riders. Even then, while conversing with the elves, he was having to think very carefully about every word he used in case the Giant's language slipped out.

"I'll give him our farewells and we can be on with it," the ranger voiced, nodding at Elderhall's high walls in the distance.

Galanör stood up, his features just as rigid as the stone beneath his boots. "Pray caution, Asher." The elf maintained his grip on Swiftling.

Crossing the edge of the knoll, the ranger was sure to make some noise as he approached the Giant. Once close enough, his towering stature eclipsed the still rising sun. Gaining no reaction, Asher cleared his throat and named the hulking man.

His mane of shaggy hair turned and a single dark eye peered down at the ranger through matted strands. "*That is not this Giant's name,*" came his profoundly low voice. "*The scar-man says Grod, so they all say Grod.*"

"*Then what is the Giant's name?*" Asher asked, his grasp on the language having crystallised.

"*Hadarax of the Oden seed.*" He slapped his chest with one mighty hand. "*Hadarax fights for the Gondolian Horde,*" he added proudly, the name lost on the ranger.

Asher held out one hand. *"Well met, Hadarax of the Oden seed. I am Asher of… Illian."*

The Giant scrutinised the extended arm and simply mimicked it without actually reaching to grip the ranger's forearm. *"Well met, Asher of Illian. Hadarax does not know of such a place."*

"It's very far from here," the ranger admitted. *"Across the sea."*

"Asher flies with Fire Snake," his indomitable voice stated.

"Avandriell," the ranger said. *"Asher's companion. Avandriell knows Hadarax's language."*

"Hmm," the Giant groaned. *"Fire Snake dropped a ship on Hadarax. Lost an eye,"* he added, pointing at his blood-streaked face.

"Sorry about that. Avandriell was trying to save Asher from the scar-man, Balthazar."

Hadarax grunted and repeated the name, his knuckles crunching into fists.

"How did Hadarax come to be a prisoner?"

The Giant looked down at him again. *"Hadarax fish on island off Glimmer Lands,"* he answered in his gruff and blunt way. *"Scar-man and little men came by boat. Hadarax ambushed. Taken to scar-man's hill in chains."*

Asher nodded, taking in the ill-fated tale. *"Well, Hadarax is free now,"* he offered hopefully. *"Hadarax hails from The Glimmer Lands, aye? The humans in this realm call it Qalanqath."* He turned to regard the south. *"That way,"* he directed. *"Stay off the roads and Hadarax will see home."*

Looking to the south, the Giant tucked up his bottom lip, pulling his chin into the grimace. *"Hadarax not for The Glimmer Lands. Hadarax for Asher of Illian."*

The ranger blinked. *"What? What does that mean?"*

"Asher save Hadarax. Hadarax must save Asher."

His understanding of the situation required an extra second to sink in. *"No,"* he said, rejecting the *debt*. *"Free now. No save,"* he added in the Giant's simple way.

The wall of muscle and hair didn't move. *"Hadarax save Asher,"* he repeated.

Shaking his head, the ranger argued, *"That's not..."* He discovered there was no word for *necessary* in their language. *"Asher came here to slay the... sea beast,"* he began again, using what vocabulary he had at his disposal. *"Big sea beast,"* he specified, using his hands to imply the scale.

The Giant grunted. *"Hadarax slay sea beast with Asher."*

"No," he rebutted.

"Hadarax slay sea beast with Asher."

The ranger opened his mouth to double down when his name was called out from across the plains. The elves were eager to return to Elderhall.

Returning his attention to the Giant, he could see that the enormous being was not to be dissuaded. Rather than attempt another line of argument, he simply pivoted and began walking back to his immortal friends. Within a few yards he was accompanied by the thundering steps of Hadarax.

"Galanör's going to love this..."

* * *

Entering Elderhall via the road, the now *four* companions passed beneath the towering arch hewn from the city's natural wall. It was an imposing entrance and crafted to such a height as to make the Giant appear small.

As it had been when arriving astride Avandriell, entering Elderhall in the company of a Giant was something of a spectacle. People emerged from every nook and cranny to lay eyes on Hadarax. While they had marvelled at Avandriell with a mix of awe and trepidation, they looked upon the Giant with fear and derision.

It didn't help that he was coated in so much dry blood.

Under so much scrutiny, however, it seemed an age before they arrived at the bridge leading to Elderhall's most grand estate. It seemed even longer that they were forced to wait, the guards unwilling to allow the likes of a Giant into Blood Lord Thalik's home.

It was eventually smoothed out when the knights from Valgala arrived on horseback—a fact that still didn't make them any taller than Hadarax. Reminding the guards of the authority granted to the elves, the path was cleared, though it was obvious that even the knights had their reservations.

The island's guards were only the first problem they encountered. For all the loftiness and open spaces of the blood lord's home, it hadn't been built with a Giant in mind. Hadarax brushed against anything and everything, knocking over antique vases, sculpted statues, and displacing ancient portraits. He successfully navigated the first passage, ducking beneath the archway, but failed to anticipate the elaborate candelabra on the other side. The shock of it staggered the Giant, who then put an elbow through a window.

"Perhaps," Galanör said pointedly, "you should show Hadarax out the back. There's a jetty and a small beach. He could clean off."

"We'll have our notes and books brought outside," Aenwyn added.

Asher thought of the struggle coming their way should the Giant attempt to enter the spirally stairwell into the archives. *"This way, Hadarax,"* he bade, breaking away from the elves.

Standing on the sandy beach, the waters stretched out to the southern curve of Elderhall's surrounding wall, where a large entrance had been cut out for ships to pass through. Dotted around the interior, numerous boats bobbed on the calm waves, their occupants enjoying a pleasant day of fishing. Those closest to the island had stopped, of course, their activity abandoned in favour of staring at the ginormous figure on the shore.

For the second time, Asher gestured at the water and urged his new companion to go and wash himself down.

"Clean?" the Giant questioned with a frown. *"Why Hadarax clean?"*

The ranger made a point to look him up and down.

"People don't usually wear other people's insides on their outside. It can be... dangerous," he said, unable to find a word for *scary* or *frightening*. Seeing the Giant's confusion, he pointed out a patch of blood on his

forearm. *"The people—they don't like this. Hadarax have to clean it off. It makes people... angry."*

Hadarax looked away, sighting some of the fishermen staring at him. He grunted once and strode towards the gentle waves. He waded in up to his waist and began cupping the water before scrubbing his arms and chest down.

It wasn't long before the house servants set up a seating area and aided the elves with moving their books and sundries to the southern veranda. Food and water was brought in abundance; at least for the likes of a human. Considerably more meat and fruit was required to appease Hadarax.

Tossing a grape into his mouth, feet elevated upon another chair, Asher looked to his elven friends. "So we can all agree that Dragon's Bane was a huge mistake, then?"

While Galanör maintained his stoical expression at the comment, Aenwyn adopted an air of irritation.

"It was a perfectly good plan that should have benefited everyone and given us the advantage against the Leviathan," she responded, her words annunciated at speed. "Were any but *Balthazar Blackhelm* sitting on that ridiculous throne we would have an armada at our disposal by now."

"Come now," Galanör replied, a light touch to his voice that suggested a mischievous remark was on the tip of his tongue. "You're forgetting about our new ally—the *Giant*." His tone dropped at the end and his eyes fell judgmentally on Asher.

The ranger glanced at Hadarax, who had remained in the water in an attempt to catch fish with his bare hands. "He might be of more use than you think. He's damn *strong*."

"And *loyal* apparently," Aenwyn commented.

"Yes," Galanör said, continuing in his previous tone. "What does Avandriell make of her new companion? She must be thrilled at the thought of having a Giant on her back."

Asher picked up an apple and took a particularly loud bite, his gaze never wandering from the elf.

"He's not our companion. He just needs to feel like he's helped me. I'm sure we can find something for him to do. Then he can be on his way."

The sound of grating armour turned the trio back to the house, where one of the knights was approaching with a missive in hand. "Ambassadors," he addressed, offering a curt bow. "Word from the port master. The ship will be ready at dawn."

"Thank you, Captain," Galanör replied, accepting the missive.

Aenwyn was nodding, the elf clearly torn between eager anticipation and dread. "We must return our efforts to the original plan."

Asher raised an eyebrow. "Which was?"

"We lure it out," she told him, "and I put an arrow between its eyes." Exaggerating her point, she placed the enchanted bow on the table.

"Good plan," Asher replied evenly. "Let's just hope it *has* eyes..."

10

THE BAIT

As the first rays of light peeked over the eastern horizon and bathed Elderhall in golden light, the ship aptly named, *The Bait*, set sail out of the harbour and beyond the ancient impact site. Manned by a skeleton crew, they took the vessel beyond the shallows and into open waters, braving the depths for a handful of miles.

From the sky, Asher looked down, between Avandriell's wing joint and scaled neck, to see the crew departing on rowboats, each set to see them returned safely to the city. By all reports, they were too small to concern the Leviathan, especially when something so large as a ship was tearing through the surface, and with the wind caught in its sails, it was pushing west with all haste.

At least it was for an hour thereafter. The winds, inevitably, died down and The Bait became a slave to the currents, taking it southward. It was hours more that Avandriell could but follow the ship and all the while with Hadarax in her claws and the trio on her back.

Still, the dragon didn't complain. Asher could feel the hunt alive in her. Her sharp eyes roamed the glassy waters, capable of piercing the surface in a way the ranger could only dream of. She spotted sharks, a shoal of great tuna, and even a pod of whales.

No Leviathan.

"When was the last time it was sighted?" Asher called over his shoulder.

"The port master claimed to have seen it," Galanör answered. "When he was a boy..."

The ranger looked back to lay eyes on the elf. "That must have been *decades* ago."

"Yes," Galanör admitted. "He said the beast hadn't been seen for near on a hundred years before that. His father's crew questioned its existence at all. The port master told us his father believed the Leviathan to have died. They went out, fishing in deep waters. They never made it back, though fragments of their ship were found on the shore weeks later."

"That's not the same thing as an actual sighting," Asher insisted, wondering himself if the sea beast was still stalking The Hox.

"You doubt it's still down there?" Aenwyn asked.

Asher considered the question. "I think that ship could be halfway to Illian by now if it had a crew," he exaggerated. "The world's a big place and these waters are connected to more oceans than just The Hox. For all we know, it's left in search of richer hunting grounds."

"I don't think so," Galanör disagreed. "I have an ill feeling just being over these waters. My instincts tell me it's down there."

Asher knew better than to question the elf's instincts, leading him to look out on those same waters. "It might be out there," he said, "but it isn't taking the bait. What are we missing?"

Aenwyn looked down and regarded the empty ship. "Of all the reports we scoured, none were doing anything out of the ordinary."

"What *were* they doing?" the ranger asked.

"Fishing mostly," she answered. "The occasional explorer."

Asher adjusted himself in his saddle, his thoughts wandering. He had baited many a monster in his time—an age-old method that was guaranteed to lure in the predator. As long as they had what the beast was known for hunting, it should rear its ugly head. And yet...

93

The bait is wrong, Avandriell stated, drawing the answer from his deliberation.

All this thing's ever done is pull down ships, Asher countered, hoping their back and forth would elucidate the issue.

Then we are presented with two options, the dragon responded. *Either, the bait is wrong or we're simply nowhere near the Leviathan. What does your gut tell you?*

Asher didn't really need to think about it. "We've got the wrong bait," he declared so the elves could hear him.

"How so?" Galanör enquired, his doubt audible.

"The Leviathan isn't hunting *ships*. I can't believe it's interested in all that *wood*."

Galanör gripped his arm, the same revelation occurring in the elf. "It wants the *crew*."

Asher looked back at him. "If we really want to bait this beast, we're going to have to convince it there's something worth eating on that ship."

The elves shared a look, silently agreeing that, despite the increased danger of being that much closer to the water, it was still the best call. With that, Avandriell banked towards The Bait and began to glide lower and lower. Following Asher's lead, Galanör and Aenwyn prepared for a rather unorthodox departure.

Hadarax was released first who, according to the dragon, had fallen asleep in her grip. The slightest squeeze was enough to wake the Giant before his unbearable weight crashed into the deck. He cried out as he rammed through the railing on the command deck and fell once more to the main deck below.

Galanör and Aenwyn dispersed like leaves dropped by an autumn branch. As one reached out and found purchase on the central mast, the other flipped in the air and grabbed hold of a sheet that ran up from the port-side railing to the rear mast. From both, the elves could climb down with cat-like ease.

Asher thought of their intentions and decided a touch of magic would impact the water, aiding in their simulation of a working crew.

Parting from Avandriell, the ranger adopted the swan dive, his arms held out to his sides. As he did when conjuring heat or fire, he imagined the very air about him shaking with life. Falling, he pulled the magic into him, drawing on it, building on it until it wrought the space around him. To the eyes of others, his image would have been distorted by ripples and the blinding light that coalesced in his right hand.

When the moment arrived, and it quickly did, the magic saved him from death, shielding him from the collision. At the same time, his right hand punched down into the deck, expelling every ounce of magic into and beyond the ship.

The deck around his landing was shattered into pieces, the wood upended and splintered like broken glass. He had been careful, however, not to blow his way through to the lower deck and compromise the vessel's integrity. Hopefully, he thought, rising from his crouch, he had just rung the dinner bell.

A shadow passed over The Bait, lifting the ranger's gaze to Avandriell. *I will keep watch from on high.*

We'll be sure to make some noise, he replied.

And so they did. For hours, the companions paced the deck. While Hadarax's footfalls were likely more than enough to attract every creature in the sea, Asher and the elves repeatedly knocked their swords and scimitars against the ship's railing. They continued their noisy routine into the night, and how clear it was, the stars emerging from every corner of the heavens.

So too did the moon emerge, a sharp crescent hanging in the sky. Its light was so strong in the dead of sea, where civilisation could not dwell. Under that stark light, Asher's broadsword came alive, the silvyr excited by the celestial body. Hadarax ceased his incessant march and looked down on the weapon, his one eye wide with child-like amazement.

"Asher has stars in his sword," he muttered in his harsh tongue.

The ranger ran his eyes over the cool metal, understanding how the Giant had made such a comparison. "Silvyr," he explained. "*Very strong, like Hadarax.*"

Asher...

Avandriell's grave tone turned his gaze to the sky. He glimpsed the dragon as she crossed the light of the moon.

What do you see?

It's what I can't see that troubles me, Avandriell replied. *All day, the ship has attracted all manner of sea life, but they're just... gone.*

Asher knew well the effect predators had on their environment. "It's here!" he called out for the others.

With great urgency, Galanör and Aenwyn rushed to starboard and looked into the dark waters. Asher moved to join them, waiting anxiously for Avandriell's next report, while Hadarax towered over them all.

Nothing.

The waters churned just as they had, its obsidian surface alight with the moon's reflection.

"What's that?" Aenwyn was pointing to the east, just off from the ship.

Asher narrowed his eyes, searching the area. They widened with revelation. "Fish," he uttered.

Rising one at a time, their numbers soon swelled to dozens and more. They were all dead. Their scaled bodies floated across the surface, carried on the waves.

"They're everywhere," Galanör stated, directing them to the stern, where a couple of larger fish rested among the dead shoal now.

Asher leaned over the rail as much as he dared, examining the fish closest to The Bait. While some bore no obvious cause of death, there were several that looked to have been partially melted, their scales still bubbling.

Keen to see his foe, the ranger stepped back and raised one hand to the starlit sky. Blinding was the light expelled from his palm. The spell launched high, arching over the waters where it lingered.

As one, they watched intently. They saw naught but dead fish.

"Where is it?" Galanör hissed.

Asher reached out for the miniature sun he had forged. He could feel it—the threads of magic that tethered him to his creation. With a single motion, he dragged it down at speed, plunging it into The Hox. Maintained by his will alone, the spell continued to burn bright, defying the water that surrounded it.

Down...

Down...

Down it drove, bringing light to the darkness. For just a moment, it winked out, the light overshadowed by something passing above it. Then it was dimmed, the orb's power providing little more than a soft hue around something truly massive gliding beneath the ship. Soon thereafter, Asher felt his spell extinguish, taken from the world by something other than his will.

The Leviathan.

Avandriell had seen it with more clarity, her lofty vantage allowing her to make out the size and shape. For the first time in their bonded life, the ranger felt his dragon's excitement wane, her rich blood cooled by the whisper of ancient dread. She had never seen anything boast of its colossal size before, its girth alone more than twice the width of the ship.

Asher thought back on the Cerbadon—the three-headed Leviathan that had risen from the foundations of Dragorn. Compared to that monster, the sea beast would be considered small. Still, it was no comfort given that they were fighting the creature in its own habitat, where it had spent millennia perfecting its hunting technique—where no man could tread.

"Look!" Galanör was pressed against the rail, his eyes fixed on the water.

It was bubbling.

His mind shared with Avandriell's, the two rangers deduced that the bubbling water was in the Leviathan's wake.

"A trail," Asher voiced.

Hell Hags, the dragon said across their bond.

Asher naturally recalled the fiends from the twelfth edition of A Chronicle of Monsters: A Ranger's Bestiary. It had been on page fifty, the original entry scribed by Veador Hemsmith. He had, of course, battled a Hell Hag or two in his time and knew well that Avandriell was referring to the dark and oily liquid the beasts deposit into the waters around them, preventing any from seeing beyond the surface.

This was much worse.

"It secretes some kind of acid into the water," he said, voicing their conclusion.

Brace yourself! Avandriell warned.

The ranger managed to grip the railing before the ship was impacted, rocking it to port. Hadarax lost his footing and tumbled across the deck, colliding with the main mast on his way. Somehow, the elves managed to remain on their feet, their bodies simply adapting to the extreme angle before The Bait levelled out again.

Asher heard it before he smelled it, his senses guiding his attention over the railing once more. The acid was already corroding the wood, creating a sizzling *hiss* on the air. The scent was acrid and put the ranger back a step.

Aenwyn darted up, onto the command deck. Her right hand flickered over one shoulder and snatched an arrow from her quiver, the projectile nocked against the bow's string with smooth ease. It didn't matter the target, a single arrow from that bow would penetrate anything.

I have it! Avandriell exclaimed.

The dragon could be seen off the bow of the ship, her bronze body tucked into a plummeting spear. At the last second, her wings unfurled and she glided across the water, her jaws stretched wide. From east to west, she ignited the sea with flames, dogging the Leviathan as it curled around The Bait.

The gargantuan black mass fell away, seeking depths unknown as Avandriell flapped her wings and gained altitude. There was some elation about the dragon, as if she had struck first blood.

I will teach it fear, she promised.

Asher never took his eyes from the water. *I don't think it's afraid.*

There came no warning upon its return. The Bait was struck on the port side, its hull brushed by the Leviathan's entire bulk as it dived up and out of the water. Asher could only glimpse the monster, its body concealed by the rolling ship, the deck having risen up like a wall.

Terror pierced his heart but not for himself, his own life saved when Galanör caught him by the hand, preventing him from falling into boiling waters. It was for Avandriell.

The Leviathan had shot up, its maw flexed to ensnare the dragon whole. Though he did not witness it, the ranger felt the event play out through his bond, making him aware of the last second manoeuvre that took Avandriell from its path. It was not enough, however, to save her from its inevitable fall.

As The Bait rocked back, tossing all four companions in the opposite direction, the Leviathan was slamming back into the The Hox, and with Avandriell trapped beneath it. The dragon was hammered by the monster's tough exterior and weighed down by its plummeting bulk.

"Avandriell!" Asher bellowed, seeing naught but the tower of water that splashed up in their wake.

The Bait was tormented by its ongoing momentum, sending them all back the other way. Asher managed to find purchase on one of the sheets tied about the main mast. Galanör drove a dagger into the deck and held himself in place while Aenwyn simply braced herself against the starboard railing.

Hadarax went *through* the railing.

The Giant cried out as he disappeared over the side, out of sight. "*Hadarax does not like the water!*" he yelled up, one meaty hand still gripped to the ship. "*Hadarax cannot swim!*"

"*What?*" Asher snapped, struggling to steady himself against the constant and unrelenting motion. "*Hadarax can't swim!*"

His disbelief was entirely set aside when he felt Avandriell's panic. He made his way across the deck, feeling her strife beneath the waves. The dragon had been freed from the monster's overbearing weight but pitted against the depths in which she had been plunged.

99

And it was coming for her.

Get out of there! he yelled across their bond.

There came no response from the dragon, all her efforts put into evading the behemoth. There was also pain. He could feel Avandriell pushing through it, doing her best to ignore the ache that ran down her right side or the sting of the acidic water.

The Leviathan was no more than a shadow moving through already dark waters, but Avandriell could see that it was circling her, watching her. Did it remember her kind? Did it remember the dragons who had run it from the land and into the cold embrace of the sea? The truth remained to be seen, leaving but a single fact: it knew only hunger.

As the dragon broke the surface and Hadarax reached up to grab the deck, the Leviathan breached the water, its huge head curling to bring its mouth down on Avandriell. It was too dark to discern the creature's appearance, only that its mouth was a black abyss of shark-like teeth. Asher could only watch, frozen against the mast, fearing that he was witnessing his companion's end.

But Avandriell was a ranger—a *monster hunter*.

Rather than put her energy into breaking the water and flying away—a potentially fatal outcome given the Leviathan's looming proximity—the dragon whipped her head around and unleashed a jet of fire. Its mouth open, the great beast tasted those scorching flames and recoiled mid-dive. Avandriell was taken down again by its weight, but she had avoided being eaten. For now.

The rocking ship carried Asher on his knees to the railing. He hardly noted the Giant's climb, bringing him back onboard. His attention was, instead, fixed on the water, desperate to see her. He could feel her held breath tight in his own chest, her every muscle working twice as hard to navigate the sea.

The beast was in her peripheral vision, circling to come back at her.

Avandriell's mighty tail propelled her up towards The Bait, where her dark claws gripped to its hull, dragging her up. At the same time, her weight balanced out the ship's rocking, allowing those with legs to stand with some ease. Asher swelled with hope to see her rise above the deck, her wings unfurling in a spray of water. Her horns were clearly damaged and the one above her left eye had snapped in half.

Quickly! she demanded, urging them to climb over her right leg.

"Everybody on!" Asher growled, waving them over.

The sea exploded, birthing the demon once more.

There was no indescribable head this time nor a gaping maw of teeth. Instead, the Leviathan unleashed seven oily black tentacles, each as thick as a tree and tipped with a bony claw. All seven of them attacked Avandriell, the claws seeking to penetrate scales and flesh alike. She roared, her rage marred by pain.

"Ava!" Asher cried, helpless but to watch as she was cleaved from the vessel and dragged into the depths.

Of all the emotions that ever churned in Asher, it was the most dangerous one that saw the ranger dive in after her, his body swallowed whole by the cold black.

Love...

11

THE BURNING SEA

All at once, Asher's senses were set alight and his environment with them. His blood forever stained by the Nightseye elixir of the Arakesh, the ranger made an ally of the pitch black. His skin adopted magnitudes of sensitivity beyond the norm, allowing his mind to build a perfect picture of his surroundings.

The Bait was just behind him, its hull slick with grime and notably damaged by the acidic water. Scattered about the ship, he could *feel* the many fish that had got caught in the Leviathan's astringent wake. That same acid lingered still, burning his skin and clothes. The ranger quickly swam for the patches of water where its presence was weakest, leaving him with the sting of its touch.

Avandriell shone brightly in his mind, her bronze scales a unique element beneath the waves. Her every motion impacted his body, informing him of her actions, her clawing and gnashing at the thick tentacles that had coiled around her.

The taste of dragon blood kissed his lips and bathed on his tongue. It was enough to draw him in, his arms and legs moving as one to close the gap. The Leviathan's presence, however, struck him like a blow.

Not since the Cerbadon had he encountered a living thing so massive in scale. Its strange body was steadily being comprised in his mind's eye.

He could *see* now that the majority of its body was one long piece of obtuse muscle, as if its structure had simply grown without any input from nature, robbing it of a single defining feature save its writhing tentacles, though even they looked to have sprouted from seemingly random places, defying the laws of symmetry that applied to any life form. Most recognisable was the creature's eyes—six bulbous globs either side of its mouth, which looked to take up most of its front half.

Those black and featureless eyes were locked onto its prey.

Avandriell.

The dragon was battling the hooked tentacles. Between their writhing and coiling, Asher detected six more limbs, all tucked against the monster's muscular hide. His acute senses required an extra moment to feel them out and make a clear picture, but he soon came to realise that they were legs and feet. Judging by the volume of slime and membranes he could unfortunately taste, he decided the limbs hadn't been used in eons and had slowly been absorbed by the body, adding to its misshapen form.

To the ranger's great anguish, he discovered nothing about the Leviathan that would help him slay it. What he could do was distract it while he still had enough air in his lungs to remain under water.

Bringing his palms within inches of each other, he ignited the spark of magic within him and began generating light.

A ripple ran through the Leviathan, its powerful muscles reacting to the shift in its attention. The tentacles cast Avandriell aside and, at the same time, propelled the monster through the water. Big as it was, the beast required a large turning circle, giving the dragon all the more time to reach the surface and take a much-needed breath.

Asher knew his companion would return in that same breath, never to abandon the fight. Until then, he faced it alone, a lamb in the shadow of a lion.

PHILIP C. QUAINTRELL

The black mass had turned to face him now and was gaining size the closer it got. He could feel its jaw opening into four different segments, a trait that gifted the Leviathan the biggest bite possible.

Elation coursed through Avandriell's body as she gulped down precious air. The dread in her bones, though, was enough to wipe such feelings away, forcing her back into a dive. Through their bond, the dragon benefitted from his heightened senses, pinpointing his location in the vast nothingness of cold water. It wouldn't matter, Asher knew. She couldn't reach him in time, the distance too great.

With naught but magic at his disposal beneath the waves, the ranger opened himself to the Realm of Magic, the source seeping out of his very bones. The light between his hands intensified, his magic beginning to build upon itself in preparation. That light was also drawing the Leviathan towards him, its enormous bulk forcing so much water around it.

NO! Avandriell screamed into their bond, seeing her companion's imminent death.

A streak of light pierced the water at an enviable speed that even the Leviathan couldn't match. The light punctured its side and the beast recoiled, its flesh blowing out into the sea in chunks, and all amidst a dark cloud of blood. It created a sickly taste in Asher's mouth, before he was pushed away by the water compressed between him and the turning Leviathan.

While the first bolt hadn't delivered a mortal blow, it had informed the monster that it could be hurt. After a sharp turn, it dived into impenetrable darkness, and only a moment before a second streak shot through the depths.

You damned fool! Avandriell growled, dipping her head under him.

Asher braced his knees and looked up, waiting for that glorious moment when his face would break the surface and he could breathe again. He inhaled as the dragon raised her head, allowing him to leap onto the deck. It had never felt so good to have something hard under his feet.

Stay on the ship! Avandriell commanded, her wings flapping hard to launch her into the sky.

Dripping wet, Asher turned to spy his companions, his senses feeling terribly dull now. There upon the command deck was Aenwyn, her bow nocked with a third arrow. She released it, sending the projectile with all the ancient power Valanis had bestowed on the bow. He watched the bright arrow thunder into the depths of The Hox, where it would continue until it found the bottom of the world.

"I can't see it!" Aenwyn complained.

Galanör froze beside the ranger, his gaze hard and so distant as to be on the horizon instead of the waters. "No," he breathed.

Asher, Avandriell intoned at the same time.

Turning to starboard, he quickly located the source of alarm and was drawn across the deck.

How many? he asked, relying on Avandriell's lofty vantage.

I count thirteen.

A low and rumbling growl resonated from deep in Hadarax's broad chest.

"*Pirates.*"

Galanör dashed to the railing and used the webbing of sheets to find elevation, his brow knotted.

"What do you see?" Asher asked.

"The lead ship," the elf replied grimly. "There stands a figure upon its bow."

"Balthazar Blackhelm," Aenwyn announced from the top of the steps, her sight just as piercing.

"He survived then," Asher remarked miserably, his chest still heaving.

Avandriell's exquisite sight closed the gap and informed the ranger that the pirate lord sported numerous fresh wounds. Still, to have survived the falling ship at all was a miracle Asher could have done without.

It's on the move! the dragon reported, a second before The Bait was jolted from below.

Asher steadied himself and looked on to see the swell of water heading towards the pirate fleet, a bubbling trail in its wake. Though distant, they could still hear roaring commands as the ships began to disperse into a new formation. Every single one of their mounted ballistas—and they were plentiful—were aimed at the waves.

The nearest six ships opened fire, releasing their flaming seven-foot bolts into the sea. They each vanished beneath the surface, all converging on almost the same location. A great splash broke the waves, revealing the sleek curves of three black tentacles as the Leviathan sought out the depths once more.

A chorus of cheers erupted from the fleet—fools. Asher's hand tightened around the railing, watching the scene intently.

Can you see it? he asked Avandriell.

The dragon paused. *No,* she eventually replied. *Wait...*

From the inky depths, they snaked up the side of a pirate ship. Cries went out across the fleet and ballistas were hurriedly repositioned. It was too late for that ill-fated ship. Three more tentacles joined the rest, only they didn't trace the hull as the others did. Instead, they rose from the sea either side and immediately coiled around the vessel, the main mast nestled between them.

Asher didn't dare blink.

It was with awe and disbelief that he watched the Leviathan snap the entire ship in half. It had the look of an implosion, its heart sucked into the water while its bow and stern were flung up towards the sky. The crew screamed in unison, thrown wild from the deck and into The Hox's dark embrace.

More bolts were launched at the beast and most of them found their mark, plunging deep into the creature's flesh. But the damage had been done, the ship reduced to pieces, its crew lost to the Leviathan's hunger, and its central mast had even fallen across the deck of another vessel, creating havoc.

"What's that?" Galanör was looking at the cluster of ships south of the formation.

Asher heard it too. Distress. Violence. Death.

Despite being nowhere near the Leviathan, the crews on those ships were entangled in some kind of battle, their silhouettes rushing about.

You're drifting towards them, Avandriell warned him.

What's happening over there? the ranger asked her.

The answer came from a quiet, yet alarming, voice in the back of his mind, an instinct that he had long learned never to ignore. His sword flicked up as he turned around, forming a horizontal barrier of silvyr between him and the fiend snapping at his throat. The force of the monster's attack rammed him into the railing, his back arching over the water.

Only inches between them, Asher got a good look at the new creature expelled by The Hox. Its flesh was that of the Leviathan's—slick and oily black. It was a skinny thing, its ribs prominent between the obsidian flesh that clung to them. Two arms and legs protruded from its narrow torso, each limb coming to three hooked claws of dull bone connected by a fine membrane.

Those claws were pressing against the silvyr blade, bringing its head closer and closer. What monstrosity it was. The majority of its skull had been given over to the mouth, its open maw so large it was capable of biting Asher's face clean off. Its vile breath assaulted the ranger as much as anything else, a rotting death he had yet to encounter in all his years.

Again and again, it snapped at him, its sloping skull as ill-defined as the Leviathan's with all its ridges and lumps. Raising his sword a notch, the creature's head was lifted atop the silvyr, angled in such a way that the ranger came eye to eye with the fiend. All three of them. Where its top jaw met its bottom jaw there sat the largest of the set, a bulbous blob of unyielding black. Curving up and back were two more eyes, each descending in size but equally as black.

It snapped at him again, revealing another three eyes on the other side of its hairless head.

Asher whipped up the hilt of his sword, bashing it about the face with the rounded pommel. The creature snarled and staggered back, numerous lids blinking rapidly across all three eyes. Undeterred, it came for him again, its clawed feet stepping towards the ranger.

Never were they to meet again, however, the beast's ghastly head taken from its bony shoulders in an explosion of gore and blood.

Aenwyn was nocking another arrow, her aim already cast elsewhere. "Scavs!" Galanör cried, his scimitars coming up.

A dozen more were climbing over the railing, their mouths parting just enough to see row after row of teeth. The moment their clawed feet touched the deck, they scattered in every direction.

Those that hoped to make a meal out of Aenwyn were the first to perish, her bow as powerful as her aim was true. The closest Scav was split apart by the magic infused arrow, its body bursting in opposite directions before the monster behind it suffered the same fate.

Galanör was a flurry of steel, the edge of his blades slicing neatly through flesh and bone alike. Swiftling dashed left, parting a Scav's head top from bottom, while Stormweaver lashed out to his right, severing another beast in half across its ribs. Both scimitars came together to meet a third, slashing in an X to reduce the creature to pieces.

The elf went on to dance and dart between the Scavs, his sword-work littering the deck with limbs and dark blood. Their chaotic nature and erratic movements, however, made it all the harder to predict their actions—and their unorthodox angles of attack. Some went high, using the mast to ascend before leaping at Galanör with claws splayed. Others almost slithered. Their bodies low to the deck so they might bite at his ankles or legs.

Asher glimpsed his old friend fall beneath two of the Scavs, his scimitars crossed to keep their clapping jaws at bay. The ranger intended to intervene, as Aenwyn had done for him, but a trio of Scavs were upon him, blocking his path to Galanör.

Evading the claws of the nearest beast, Asher pivoted and swept his broadsword round to cleave the head of another. The silvyr twisted in his grip, reversing the direction of its tip to plunge into the torso of that first fiend.

The third and last to reach him raked its claws across his shoulder, the force of its blow turning him about where it then landed a second swipe across his chest. While his shoulder was saved by the pauldron of bronze dragon scales, his pale shirt tore as easily as the skin beneath, streaking him with three lines of scarlet. The ranger growled with pain, that oldest of friends. It was not to slow him, though, only spur on the Scav's end.

It ducked beneath his wild backhand and dashed to the side, its arm extended to rake another set of red lines across his chest again. It found only the bite of silvyr, the blade delivered with enough power behind it to chop the beast's arm off at the elbow. It hissed and recoiled as it transitioned from predator to prey.

A short leap, his arm cocked back and high, Asher came down on the Scav with a thrusting blow, ploughing the broadsword through its mouth and out the other side.

The ranger quickly discovered that Galanör had never required his aid, the elf already back on his feet with a growing number of corpses about him.

Standing her ground on the command deck, Aenwyn had swapped bow for scimitar. While her cloak and leathers looked to have suffered claw marks, the elf appeared free of injury. The same could not be said of the creatures hounding her. Those that yet lived bore gashes born of elven steel, scars that would mar them for life were they not destined for death.

Something akin to a rockslide erupted from deep inside Hadarax's chest, a roar no man could match. It was accompanied by the sound of splitting flesh and pouring liquid.

Asher turned swiftly with his broadsword in both hands, his swing readied to take heads from shoulders, when he laid eyes on the Giant. Skinny as the Scavs were, Hadarax was able to get one hand around its torso and the other hand around its legs. As a being so strong as a Giant is wont to do, he pulled yet another Scav in half.

Showered in blood and gore, Hadarax threw himself into a group of Scavs. The impact was felt by all, though not so strongly as it was felt by the Scavs beneath the Giant. He writhed left and right, slamming his fists and hammering his head into anything that moved. Pulverised, there was soon nothing left resembling the creatures, leaving Hadarax drenched in dark gore.

The last of the Scavs fell from on high, the beast having surveyed from the central mast and sighted Asher as its victim. The ranger hadn't seen the monster, but he had heard its claws detaching from the wood.

In two hands, the silvyr broadsword required a simple flick, cutting through the air in a sharp arc. It also cut through the Scav's gaunt hips, slaying the creature before it even hit the deck.

Asher... Avandriell called, turning his attention back to Balthazar's fleet.

Two more ships had been destroyed by the Leviathan, their remains littering the waves. Of the remaining ten vessels, one appeared a ghost, its crew slaughtered by the Scavs, and another had been set ablaze in their defence against the creatures. The pirate lord now fought the behemoth with eight ships and six times as many ballistas, the latter of which had proved ineffective thus far.

The Leviathan surfaced in the north, its ridged body curling as it broke the waves. As it did, Asher witnessed a dozen more Scavs peeling away from its back. They disappeared briefly, taken by the water, before they could be seen climbing up the starboard hull. Then came the screaming, their hunt of the Leviathan forgotten in the face of nightmarish terrors.

It was all so easy to see now that The Bait had drifted into their midst. So much so, in fact, that they were bound for an imminent collision.

Asher braced himself against the nearest sheet. "Get ready!" he yelled, warning the elves.

The pirates too were shouting over the mayhem, desperately trying to steer their ship from calamity. There was nothing any of them could do. Both vessels came together, The Bait's bow ramming into the pirates' port side. The knock was jarring, dropping all but Hadarax to their knees momentarily.

As the two ships became one, their hulls crashing together, side by side, the Giant became an immediate problem for the pirate crew. His size and reputation made them forget that which they had come to hunt, turning their arrows and spears on him.

Hadarax roared as he charged towards them, his effortless leap taking him easily from one ship to the other. He landed with a spear in his shoulder and a cluster of arrows up his left leg and hip, though none slowed the Giant.

"Their ship has less holes," Asher remarked, running in Hadarax's wake.

"For now," Galanör replied dryly, eyeing the devastation already wrought by the Giant.

Together, the three companions jumped over the combined railing of both ships and made to commandeer the pirate vessel. Balthazar's men then faced the hardest choice of their lives: stay and fight a vengeful Giant or jump overboard and try to swim to another ship before the Leviathan dragged them down.

Picked up by his legs, one pirate was swung around so fast he didn't have the air to scream before Hadarax beat him into the mast. Death was mercifully instantaneous. The same could not be said of his shipmate, who was quickly snatched from his feet by the Giant and slowly squeezed into oblivion.

It was inevitable that Asher would clash with the crew as well. He deflected their uncoordinated attacks using muscle memory alone and, ultimately, killed two men in one fluid motion that brought his sword round and back again, opening up the gut of one before slicing across the chest cavity of the other.

Having witnessed his prowess, the archer facing him hesitated. Feeling threatened by the ranger's advance, however, he still found the courage to let go of his bowstring. The arrow was off-centre, but it would still have sank deep into Asher's arm had he not chopped it down mid-flight. That was enough to convince the man he would fare better in the water. His bow abandoned, the pirate turned and dived over the side of the ship.

He couldn't have been more unfortunate.

The Leviathan itself was rising as he met the sea. Subsequently, the pirate was brought back to the surface upon the monster's vast back. His scream was unlike any that had yet to ring out that night.

Asher looked down, watching the Leviathan curl back into the deep, as the man succumbed to the acid that bubbled the water around him. He was soon without working limbs, his skin reduced to little more than viscous slough. As such, he disappeared beneath the dark surface, his death all too slow.

The moment was broken by the impact of a ballista bolt. Asher was taken aback and all the more when one of the Leviathan's tentacles whipped out of the water in retaliation. The thick appendage swept across the deck, unaware that the bolt had come from a different vessel. The ranger managed to use the rail to gain some height and leap over the tentacle as it ripped the deck beneath him to shreds.

Landing amongst the debris, Asher was relieved to see the elves had executed a similar manoeuvre and avoided certain death. Hadarax alone had been lucky enough to have been at the stern, where the tentacle failed to reach before returning to the sea.

With a ragged leg in one hand—torn free from its owner—the Giant surveyed the wreckage, his one eye looking only for the ranger. His expression was so hidden by his tangled beard, matted hair, and no lack of blood that it was impossible to say if he was relieved as well.

Whatever his mood, it was short-lived when a ballista bolt took him from his feet.

12

THE BATTLE OF THE HOX

The Giant's name exploded from Asher's lips as he ran for the stern, taking the steps up to the command deck two at a time. Hadarax was slumped against the port side hull, the force of the bolt having pushed him partially through the ship wall.

Before approaching the Gondolian Giant, who was staring in bewilderment at the bolt protruding from his gut, Asher turned to trace the missile's path. There he discovered its origin, launched from a ballista in the very control of Balthazar Blackhelm.

Maniacal was the pirate lord's toothy grin.

Of the three ballistas lining the port side of his ship, it was the only one that had been redirected from the water. That was until he gave the command to unleash their next salvo on the adjacent vessel.

"Incoming!" the ranger cried.

Two more bolts burst from their housing along the ballistas central groove. One whistled through the air, a promise of death for Galanör. Boldly, the elf had taken to a dead sprint *towards* the missile. It seemed an impossible feat, and yet he still evaded the bolt by sliding on his knees across the deck, his head and back arched so he appeared almost horizontal. The bolt went on to destroy a portion of the railing before sinking beneath the waves.

The other bolt had Asher in its sights.

The ranger had a plethora of physical abilities at his disposal—all of which had been enhanced since bonding with Avandriell—but none could take him from the path of a ballista bolt under such close proximity. In the same vein as the Dragon Riders of old, though, Asher had *other* abilities.

And so his hand came up, fingers folding into a knot. He knew not the ancient words or the exact spells used by mages to conjure a shield, for he had no need of them, his connection to the Realm of Magic more intuitive than theirs.

It was, however, just too late.

The bolt came for him while the shield was still immature, its strength no match for the missile.

Fortunately, magic was not his only ally.

With senses and speed that dwarfed the ranger's, Avandriell shot between the two ships and snatched the bolt in her front right claws.

Kill the pirate and be done with him, the dragon said, releasing the bolt from her grip. *Three more ships have perished. The Leviathan will have its fill and you'll be stranded in the water. We must slay the beast!*

King Blackhelm was barking orders, demanding that the ballistas be reloaded and aimed at Avandriell. The fool. He would waste resources by trying to kill the only ally that could actually make a difference to his survival.

They're targeting you, Asher warned her.

Then they will meet the next life with my name on their lips.

The bronze dragon banked sharply, bringing her back around to fly over the mess of ships and debris. She was lined up perfectly to pass over Balthazar's vessel and the pirate lord saw her coming. The wretch didn't even bother to alert his crew. He shoved any and all aside as his feet took him as fast they could to the bow of the ship.

Asher disagreed that true survivors always had a portion of luck on their side, believing that it was skill and ability that made one a survivor, but damned if Blackhelm didn't have luck just sitting on his shoulder.

The pirate lord deftly navigated the bowsprit, displaying his many years as a capable sailor, and leaped, arms outstretched. He should have met the sea and a watery death, but he found purchase on the side of a passing ship—Sundancer by the name painted on its hull. As he clambered up, Avandriell unleashed fiery hell upon the ship he had departed. A single strafe torched the vessel from stern to bow, creating another blazing ship on the dark waters.

Hadarax's grunting turned the ranger around. The Giant defied the mortal blow and, somehow, staggered to his feet. The bolt was still inside him, having pierced his back to protrude beside his spine. A ragged cough escaped him and he splattered the deck with blood, his lips ruby red now.

"*Hadarax needs to rest,*" Asher insisted, gesturing for the Giant to sit down.

"*Hadarax save Asher,*" came the predictable reply.

The ranger would have argued had the Leviathan not jolted the ship and knocked them both to the deck. A pair of thick tentacles uncoiled from the sea, their claws driving into the starboard of the hull. Looking between the strands of hair that had fallen across his face, Asher watched Aenwyn skip and dart across the ship, not to be brought down by the attack.

Mid-leap, the elf let another arrow fly. The streak of light intercepted one of the tentacles and released the energy it had been storing. The limb exploded, spraying dark blood in every direction.

A sound unlike anything Asher had ever heard reverberated up through the ship as the Leviathan expressed its pain. Had it ever suffered such a wound?

The top half of the tentacle flopped onto the deck of the ship, completely separated from the monster. As its weight slowly dragged it back down into the sea, the clawed end scraped across the planks.

"Hit it again!" Asher yelled.

Vengeful, the other tentacle rose above the deck in search of victims. Aenwyn dived aside before it plunged into the ship, the claw driving through to the floor below. Again and again it hammered the deck, forcing Aenwyn and Galanör to weave and dive between the impacts. Their elusive nature only brought more tentacles into the fight. Varying in size, they probed the hull until they found the edge of the railing, their claws tapping at the wood.

The elves, however, knew exactly how to work together.

Galanör skidded beneath one sweeping tentacle, one hand whipping out to scoop up a fallen arrow. Flipping back to his feet, he leaped and somersaulted over another black limb before tossing the arrow into the air.

Simultaneously, Aenwyn was rebounding off the central mast—evading a claw almost as tall as herself. The elf caught the arrow between her fingers and nocked it while still moving through the air.

The moment her boots touched down, the arrow scorched the night, its path taking it perfectly between the snaking coils to find the largest of the tentacles. The air snapped and Leviathan flesh and gore exploded in every direction. That nightmarish howl sounded again from the deep and the slick limbs withdrew from the pirate ship.

It's moving north, Avandriell reported, her flight path altering accordingly.

The dragon swooped down and blanketed the waves in fire before her flames ran over another vessel. The pirates cried out, fleeing the extreme heat, but they had nowhere to go.

As if to make itself feel better, the Leviathan emerged north-west of the blazing ship, where one of the smaller vessels sailed on the edge of the battle. Its clawed tentacles lashed out of the waves and seized the ship, tearing it to pieces while more Scavs peeled off its exposed back.

Avandriell descended at speed, the claws on all four of her feet splayed. Asher filled their bond with feelings of caution but the dragon was already upon the great monster, her impatience winning out.

Avoiding the many ballista bolts sticking out of it, every one of her claws sank to the knuckle, biting into Leviathan hide. The creature writhed and its tentacles forgot about the pirate ship. At the same time, Avandriell's wings flapped hard, her feet curling to maintain her grip on the fiend.

For all her strength there was no shifting the beast, its weight simply too much, and for all her effort, Avandriell gained only *pain*.

"No!" Asher bellowed.

The dragon's agony was blinding, her feet subjected to the Leviathan's natural acids. Avandriell had no choice but to return to the sky, leaving sixteen deep gouges in its back. She did so only a second before its tentacles would have enveloped her.

Asher watched her ascend, smoke drifting from her feet. She was in too much pain to communicate anything intelligible, but the ranger could feel her rage bubbling beneath the agony of the acid's touch.

"Is she alright?" Galanör asked, arriving at Asher's side.

"She's not out of the fight yet," Asher uttered, his gaze pausing on the thick clouds rolling over the world.

A storm was coming.

"Nor is he apparently," the elf remarked, eyeing the Giant rising beside them.

Hadarax stumbled before his hand gripped the ship's wheel and he managed to balance himself. No easy feat with a ballista bolt in his gut. On her way up the steps to the command deck, Aenwyn released another arrow into the night. It illuminated the surface of the waves before its light died inside the Leviathan itself, sending chunks of the ancient beast high into the air. The monster shuddered and ceased its distant attack in favour of the deep once more.

"This thing won't die!" Aenwyn complained.

Hadarax took one end of the bolt in both hands and began to yank it free.

"No!" Asher blurted, dashing to stop him. "*Leave it! Hadarax will bleed to death!*"

"*Hadarax does not fear death,*" the Giant replied miserably.

"*How will Hadarax save Asher if Hadarax is dead?*" the ranger countered.

"It's coming this way!" Aenwyn warned them.

Asher turned from the Giant and spotted the swell of water. It *was* coming for them, and with all speed.

"Brace yourselves!" the ranger yelled, though the impact never occurred. Avandriell tore out of the sky, her fiery breath leading the way. While the flames failed to penetrate the water, they did lick at the Leviathan's back as it crested the waves. Its tentacles flicked up and curled round as it, again, descended beyond the dragon's reach.

The spectacle of her interference, however, proved a distraction from another impact that could not be prevented.

Asher swore, seeing the calamity all too late.

Two ships—one under the command of Balthazar Blackhelm—rammed into their commandeered vessel, pinching it simultaneously on the starboard bow and port side stern. The resulting crash brought all three ships together, their hulls slamming into each other until they were lined up side by side and slowly rotating with their combined momentum.

All, including Hadarax, were taken clean from their feet and hurled across the ship. Asher felt every one of the steps as he tumbled limb over limb, down to the main deck, his broadsword clattering along with him.

Sprawled and injured, there was so much noise bombarding the ranger from all sides. The roar of fires and an enraged dragon. Cries of pain and death—of *fear*. The snapping and splintering of wood across all three ships, their sheets becoming entangled and sails ripping. The distinct sound of steel, of swords being drawn.

Added to all of that, the storm had caught up with them. What had started as the light tapping of water droplets quickly became relentless sheets of cold rain.

The hollers came from either side, where pirates were making the short leap from one ship to another. They did so on the orders of King Blackhelm, who was among the last to depart Sundancer and jump onto Asher's vessel.

Not to be defeated by a few steps, the ranger picked himself up with a grunt and white knuckles about the hilt of his silvyr sword. *Kill the pirate and be done with him*, Avandriell had said. It would have been so simple a thing were there not two dozen men between them.

First blood, however, was not to be Asher's. Aenwyn slid down the bannister from the command deck, her right arm working furiously to draw arrow after arrow. Fired from Adellum's bow, each missile killed more than a single target, blasting ragged holes in their bodies, and bringing her tally to six before the elf had even set foot on the main deck.

Asher was by her side as she swapped bow for scimitar and met the rushing pirates. While their fighting prowess was lacking, Balthazar's men had the numbers, and within seconds of clashing with them in combat, they had all the angles.

What they didn't have, was a *Galanör*.

The elf leaped over the railing, Stormweaver and Swiftling in his hands. Landing in their midst, he was a storm unto himself, his winds that of steel and death.

While steel and silvyr rang out, the pirate lord was redirecting a handful of his men to the mounted ballistas—he wanted to turn the combined ships into a floating fort against the Leviathan. That was not all they were to bring down. The ballistas that couldn't take aim at the water anymore, their path blocked by the parallel ships, were repositioned to roam across the sky—what they could see of it, at least. The rain lashed and sporadic flashes of lightning made a mockery of the heavenly scape, but they offered Avandriell some much-needed cover.

For just a second, the rain failed to find the ship and two of the ballistas fired their bolts into the air, chasing the bronze dragon.

It infuriated Asher, more so than if it had been aimed at his own heart. By the edge of his broadsword, the ranger broke through the wing of oncoming pirates and dashed for the nearest interior ballista. A short leap and a swift thrust impaled the man reloading the bolts, pinning him to the framework of the wooden machine itself. Keeping his movements fluid, Asher pivoted and drew the silvyr short-sword from over his right shoulder. The pirate who had been operating the trigger failed to retrieve his sword before he lost everything above his jawline.

"Scavs!" Galanör bellowed.

Asher yanked his broadsword free of the ballista and turned to see the truth of it. The damned beasts were clambering over the ships that had wedged his own, their glassy black flesh glistening in the fires that dotted the seas.

Night became day as Avandriell swept past the ship-fort, her fiery breath igniting Sundancer's port side from end to end. A dozen Scavs were removed from the battle before they could even get into it, but those that advanced from the other ship were already hurtling themselves over the railings and onto the companions' ship. They stretched their enormous mouths and shrieked in a display of sharp teeth.

Avandriell glided past again, this time bringing her fire down on the other side of the ship-fort, walling it off on both sides with flames. It would reduce the Scavs again but it did nothing to deal with those now throwing themselves into the fray. Nor did it help the dragon herself, who had caught the Leviathan's attention.

Asher decapitated one Scav and gutted another before his eyes cast out beyond the wall of flames, on the starboard side. He watched as massive tentacles erupted from the water, their claws biting into Avandriell's hide and through the membranes of her wings. She was prevented from flying away before being dragged down to the sea, where the bulk of the Leviathan's body soon appeared. Through their bond, Asher knew that its mouth had peeled back like the petals of a flower, allowing it to extend the size of its bite.

"Ava!" the ranger cried.

As his short-sword slotted back into its sheath on his back, the broadsword flicked up and round to split another Scav in half, clearing his path to Avandriell.

The dragon roared in defiance, her pained feet clawing at the Leviathan in a bid to combat the tentacles.

Asher could see that open maw in his mind's eye. An abyss that would swallow his immortal companion almost whole. A black hell that would take her from him.

That spark—that soul-crushing thought—ignited a plethora of emotions in the ranger. It was enough to excite his very skin with the touch of magic, raw as it was. With no clear thought as to how he might mould the magic, how he might refine it into useable spells, it began to manifest as pure energy, amplified by his connection to a dragon—a being of magic.

Without realising, he had crossed from one ship to another, his feet taking him at speed towards Avandriell. He could see her through the flames, wrestling with a creature from history's darkest nightmares. Bowing her head, the dragon looked down the throat of the monster and reminded it why her kind were so revered, if not feared.

The jet of fire found every inch of the Leviathan's mouth, the flames spreading to scorch as much flesh as possible. The great fiend thrashed, its tentacles and main body slamming into the ship-fort.

Asher was taken from his feet and the central mast was snapped like a twig after Avandriell was momentarily rammed into it. The ranger managed to roll sideways, evading the column of wood before it could crush him.

Still feeling the warm breath of magic on the back of his neck, Asher picked himself up, his broadsword scraping over the ruined deck.

Avandriell remained in the Leviathan's grip, the beast having briefly submerged to extinguish the flames that had tortured it. Some ancient vendetta seemed to rule the demon, making it determined to consume the dragon, for those horrendous jaws unfurled once more.

The ranger didn't know what he was going to do, but he knew he would put himself between Avandriell and that maw. His moment of action, however, was taken from him, robbed by that most wretched of pirates.

Balthazar Blackhelm had leaped from the fallen mast, his boot ramming into Asher's side. The force of it was enough to stagger the ranger and threaten his footing. He might have recovered and tried again to save Avandriell had the pirate lord not come at him with axe and sword.

Asher... Avandriell's voice was strained.

For the first time in her life, she was fighting a creature that boasted more strength than her own. Asher could feel the dragon's shock, the terrifying bewilderment—the revelation—that she wasn't the apex predator she thought she was. Since the defeat of Malliath, the dragon had never thought to look Death in the eye.

The same could not be said of the ranger, who had walked hand-in-hand with death since he was an Outlander in The Wild Moores.

He met Balthazar's attacks with a flurry of defences, his tactics deliberately repositioning their duel so he might aid Avandriell before it was too late.

But it *was* too late.

Asher felt his companion's alarm as her struggle against the Leviathan was faltering, her strength waning as more tentacles coiled about her neck and limbs. She was going to die.

Bleak and terrible was the pit that tore through Asher, a gaping wound in his soul that would never heal. It promised black days to his very last, making a ruin of every fine day to come.

Thunderous steps pounded the deck.

Hadarax shoved past Asher and Balthazar with speed and strength unbefitting of one with a ballista bolt lodged inside their gut. So too was his roar powerful, a defiant cry in the face of certain death.

There had been no stopping the Giant, just as there would have been no stopping a charging bull with bare hands.

All at once, Hadarax jumped through the fires that licked the port side and pulled free the ballista bolt from his gut. Asher yelled his name but it was lost to the storm and warring behemoths.

The Giant missed the Leviathan's opening mouth and fell upon the seam where two of the four jaws came together. It was also where three of the monster's six eyes were situated.

Hadarax brought the bolt down with both hands and obliterated all three bulbous domes.

The Leviathan forgot about Avandriell in an instant, slamming her into the water before its tentacles uncoiled and its claws detached. The entire ship-fort was rocked as the beast moved away, its bulk rising to test the strength of the ship's hull.

The Giant was still fixed to its side, his hands clamped around the bolt he had plunged into the eyes. He was also on his knees and wailing in agony. Smoke was rising from his melting skin, yet he would not let go of the bolt. If anything, he yanked it violently from side to side, delivering as much damage as he could before he met his watery end.

"Hadarax!" Asher bellowed.

Turned on its side now and seeking the comforts of the deep, the Leviathan began to disappear beneath the waves, its remaining tentacles and stumps following in its wake.

It took Hadarax of the Oden seed with it, the Giant who had saved Avandriell from the promise of death.

Asher was powerless to do anything but watch through the pouring rain and dragon fire, his respect and admiration for Hadarax crystallising in his heart for all time.

Further out, the sea exploded and Avandriell found flight again. The sight of her flooded Asher with the hope needed to combat the grief he felt for Hadarax's sacrifice, though there was no time to mourn the Giant.

The pirate lord was coming for his head.

The ranger ducked beneath the swinging axe and rolled backwards, giving himself some space before the next attack.

He glimpsed his foe's feet leaving the deck as he rose from the evasion and instinctively lifted the broadsword to block the incoming blow. While the weight of the attack was enough to bring Asher's blade down, the pirate's subsequent backhand was too slow to remove the ranger's head.

A solid shoulder-barge put the pirate back a step and a boot to the chest put Blackhelm flat on the deck. Asher hefted his broadsword and waited for the fool to pick himself up—he wouldn't sully the fine blade by stabbing the man while he was on his back.

Drenched by the rain, Balthazar's lopsided copper hair was plastered over the burn scars that marred so much of his scalp. There was no hiding his other scars, all proudly displayed by the shirtless pirate.

Up close, Asher could see the new wounds he had gained when Avandriell dropped a ship on his home. Most obvious was his right eye, which had lost all its white in place of red and was haloed by severely damaged skin. The hands that gripped his axe and sword possessed numerous fingers that had been strapped together by the same type of bandaging that bound his chest and portions of his arms. Even so, the extent of some of his injuries escaped the limitations of the bandages, revealing deep gashes that would go on to scar—if he was to go on living.

Balthazar sniffed loudly and began to slowly retreat, his steps taking him back towards the central ship, where the conflict continued between the three parties.

"You're not the first Dragon Rider to try and bring me down!" he growled at the ranger, beating his chest. "The Dawning Isles are mine! The Hox is mine!"

The pirate tripped over some debris as he navigated the fallen mast, his sword quickly coming up to point at Asher.

He was afraid.

It was there to see in his eyes. He was trying to use anger to drown it out, to bolster his frayed nerves and lend him the courage required to defeat a warrior worthy of the dragon heart. But he saw what everyone saw when they looked at Asher.

That unyielding tide that could not be bartered with.

That reckless pursuit that always saw the predator catch its prey.

That undeniable danger that clung to his very person.

"You think because you have a dragon, you get to decide how the world works! Who sits on the thrones! Who wears the crowns! Not here!" Balthazar raged, his retreat blocked where the ships had become stuck together.

Beyond him, Galanör and Aenwyn were all that remained of those who had faced the Scavs. Still, they danced and weaved between the littered corpses of dead pirates and brought their wrath against the Leviathan's beastly pets.

"I am a king!" Balthazar proclaimed. "It is my *right* to take what I want!"

"You already had everything!" Asher yelled back at him. "But you lost it all the moment you tried to kill her."

So swift was the ranger it seemed he was in two places at once, his sword both resting by his leg and whipped out to the side.

All too late did the pirate lord realise who the ranger was talking about, and so his look of understanding was tarnished by the shock of the broadsword that ran across his throat.

His axe and sword released from his grip, Balthazar Blackhelm fell to his knees with his hands pressed against the bleeding wound that tore through his neck. Eyes glassy and bulging, he looked up at Asher in disbelief, as so many did when they were on the precipice of death. The expression was not to last.

Wielded in both hands, the silvyr broadsword swept from right to left, cleaving the pirate lord's head from his shoulders. Thus ended the reign of the pirate king, Balthazar Blackhelm.

Asher wouldn't give him a second thought.

13

TIMELINE

The entire ship-fort was shaking. The ranger braced himself and remained on his feet, but the destruction rippling through all three conjoined ships was only just beginning.

Again and again, the central ship succumbed to a quake that looked to be tugging the entire vessel down. Bit by bit, pieces of the interior could be heard from the deck as the levels within were subjected to something powerful and unquestioningly violent. The hulls scraped against each other and the masts wobbled, their sheets becoming all the more tangled.

"It's the Leviathan!" Galanör cried, retrieving Stormweaver from the corpse of a Scav.

Aenwyn slotted her scimitar into its scabbard and took her bow in hand. "It's beneath us!"

Asher hopped over the two sets of railings as the central ship was dragged down another notch, staggering his landing. Without any real words, he was also calling out to Avandriell.

We cannot abandon the fight, the dragon responded, sensing his intentions. *The beast must die!*

There was a degree of retribution skewing Avandriel's perspective—perhaps more than a degree given the many wounds she bore and level of pain she was in.

We're not abandoning the fight, Asher told her, reframing the argument. *We're surviving the fight so we can return and kill it!*

The ranger hurried to meet the elves, the rain cleansing his fine sword of Blackhelm's crimson blood. "We need to get out of—"

His next words were taken from his lips just as quickly as the deck was taken from his feet. As all three companions met the planks, a pair of tentacles exploded from below, tearing through the ship by the point of their claws. They hammered down and raked at the deck, ripping through the wood like parchment until they fell through to the lower levels. They were swift to return, however, rising once again to coil around the mast and reduce it to splinters.

"Move!" Galanör shouted.

The trio dived to one side and avoided death by raining debris. Aenwyn was momentarily buried beneath one of the sails before the Leviathan's thick limbs violently swept it away, flinging the wreckage and detritus into the sea. Galanör gripped her by the forearm and yanked her to safety, saving her from the enormous claw that thundered through the very spot where she had been crawling.

"Avandriel!" Asher bellowed into the storm.

The ship was, again, dragged down, its centre gutted in such a way that its bow and stern were partially lifted from The Hox. The three companions reached out for anything that could prevent them from sliding down the fractured deck and into the bubbling water that now sat in the heart of the ship-fort.

Galanör found purchase by the grip of a single hand before Aenwyn caught his leg and Asher her's.

The ranger came to a stop only feet in front of the rising water. From the acidic depths there emerged a pointed mountain of black, the tip of the Leviathan's hideous mouth. All four jaws peeled back, flowering to rest against the shattered deck. Its innumerable teeth bristled, waiting for its prey to slide down the upturned bow and fall into the oblivion it had created.

The stench alone was enough to test the trio's resolve. How many eons had that mouth been consuming all manner of life? All that death was laid bare now while its tentacles kept it braced into position against the other ships.

"I can't hold us!" Galanör growled, his hand slipping on the wet fixing.

Asher thought to let go and lighten the load, giving the the elves the chance to climb up, but he knew what was coming. "Hang on!" he called back.

From out of the black and stormy night, Avandriell arrived as a silhouette against a flash of lightning. Her roar overshadowed the thunder that followed and her landing created an almighty crash that drowned even that out. Without a care for the already broken vessel, the dragon brought all four of her feet down on what she could of the bow section, rending it from the Leviathan's grip.

The companions yelled out as they now slid in the opposite direction, away from the voracious beast.

While her back legs were plunging into the sea, the sinking bow beneath her, Avandriell pressed her snout to the ruined deck, allowing all three of them to come to a sudden stop and clamber over her head. Beyond her three crowning horns, they navigated her blunt spinal bones and partially fell into place around the saddle.

Get us out of here, Ava!

Avandriell didn't need the mental command to flex her wings and flap with all her might. The sharp tips of her wings splashed against the water's surface and her tail hammered the waves as the dragon ascended from the wreck. One more flap of her wings and Avandriell bowed her head, determined to have the last word.

Asher and the elves shielded their eyes from the light of her fire, the flames swallowed by the Leviathan. The ancient creature brought all of its jaws together and immediately dropped beneath the surface, its anguish resonating through its thick hide.

Still in pain, Avandriell was satisfied with her farewell and made to fly off, over the remains of the stern.

But the Leviathan was never satisfied.

There came no warning of its attack but attack it did. The black waters, lashed with heavy rain, erupted in four different places, each birthing one of the Leviathan's indomitable tentacles. They coiled around Avandriell's back legs and tail, pitting the two in a battle of wills.

The dragon's strength brought a portion of the Leviathan into view, its beastly mouth appearing once more and directly beneath them. The jaws flowered and the great void of its throat looked up at them.

It's too strong, Avandriell raged, her joints working furiously to bat her wings.

The dragon roared in pain when one of the larger tentacles coiled enough to stab its clawed end into her thigh.

Try as she might, Avandriell was steadily sinking.

Asher gripped his saddle in one hand and braced himself to look down and lay eyes on the demon. It was hunger made manifest. It was vengeance personified. It was Death made flesh.

It was everything he had stood against since walking away from Nightfall.

Bringing an end to its reign over The Hox was more than just a job, it was his calling in life. Avandriell, however, *was* his life. Threatening her was enough to ignite that dangerous spark in him. That recklessness.

No, the dragon said, the word pushed through her exertion.

It's the only way, Asher replied, thinking of the same sacrifice Hadarax had just made.

Of course, the ranger had no ballista bolt to bring against the fiend. What *he* had was so much worse.

There are... consequences, Avandriell warned, her head pointed to the sky in a desperate attempt to reach it.

The ranger thought of Adilandra Sevari, the once queen of Ayda and mother to Reyna. By Doran and Faylen's report, the elf had once used her raw magic to beat back an entire horde of Sandstalkers, saving both her people and the dwarves in their company. She had survived

129

such a drastic feat and her magic returned in part before her death on Qamnaran.

She was an elf of a thousand years! Avandriell snapped, her anger lending the dragon an ounce more strength.

I won't let this thing be the end of you, the ranger told her, sighting more tentacles rising from the deep.

Asher—

The dragon's protests fell away just as Asher did. His plan could never have been guessed by the elves and so they could only look on it in utter shock as the ranger dropped towards that open mouth.

The fall felt an eternity.

His fury burned hot all the while, his bond with Avandriell allowing him to feel her pain, her sense of impending doom. The Leviathan could not have known that Asher would scorch all the earth in her defence, that he would annihilate anything and everything that threatened to take her from him.

It was a lesson to be learned all too late by his foe.

By the time he was engulfed by the darkness beyond its flowered jaws, his bones were pouring out so much magic it was as if he occupied both Verda and the Realm of Magic simultaneously. He went from being a conduit to a beacon of magic that would have been felt by any and all who could sense the breach in the veil between worlds.

There was no sudden stop, no bottom to that dreadful throat that had swallowed him whole.

Only light.

Cocooned by the ethereal forces, Asher came to a halt somewhere inside the Leviathan, where he used his rage to channel the Realm of Magic. If there was any sound it could not reach the ranger in the heart of the expulsion. Nor was there any feeling, his skin numb and muscles seized by the event.

But he welcomed it.

Encouraged it.

Demanded it.

It was intoxicating, to have such power—enough to change the world. It was limitless, an unending force that could reshape the realm as *he* saw fit.

Asher…

Avandriell's voice broke through the finest of cracks in the display of raw magic. She poured so much into his name. Her love for him. Her need of him to survive the ordeal. Her warning that he was in command of forces not meant to be meddled with, neither by mortal or immortal.

Asher pushed her out, her voice sucked into a void.

He would see it through to the end.

He would slay the Leviathan.

He would save her.

Despite the fact that he couldn't hear himself, the ranger was convinced he was roaring with the power of a thousand, thousand storms. He intensified the flow of magic squeezing through the realms, turning the light being expelled from the monster's throat into something substantial.

Into something violent.

Only seconds before it could close its jaws about Avandriell's tail—spelling her end—the magic expanded well beyond Asher, pushing out into The Hox. The Leviathan was hardly a barrier between it and the water, the monster's thick, black hide bursting apart like a sack of wine. The sea around it, and all the debris and broken ships that floated therein, were thrown in every direction, carried on one massive wave.

And all with chunks of Leviathan, the giant globs of flesh and gore hurtling through the air, destined to be no more than fish food.

Asher's light vanished with all the speed it had arrived, plunging him in darkness and frigid sea water. He was cast around in the swirl as The Hox settled back into its original shape. Gone was the magic that had insulated him, as if he had been cut off from an entire sense.

He had also lost every ounce of energy in his muscles. The surface could have been an inch from his face and still be beyond his reach, though he couldn't even guess as to which direction it could be found.

He simply existed, his body weighed down by the weaponry fixed to his various belts and straps.

The world darkened all the more as he slipped into the ocean's numbing embrace. He would be gone soon, succumbing to the fits that accompanied the lack of air. The ranger thought only of Avandriell, who would live now.

Forever.

He could die well knowing that fact.

As ever, it seemed, Death would not suffer his presence in the afterlife.

A winged angel soared through the depths of the sea, passing just beneath him. Hands grasped at him in the dark, pulling him closer. From one world to another, the ranger's eyes opened to see his transition from water to air as Avandriell broke the waves and flapped her wings. In the grips of Galanör, he was secured by elven strength.

Barely conscious, he looked down at what had been their battleground. None of Balthazar's ships had survived, his fleet decimated by Leviathan and dragon alike. Only a few flames remained, those that had survived the expulsion of magic, but their light revealed fleshy fragments of the ancient monster. A tentacle here, a hunk of hide there. It had been obliterated.

We did it, he said weakly into his bond with Avandriell.

There came no reply.

He knew when the dragon was choosing to ignore him, her response simply withheld. That was not the case now. Asher voiced her name again and knew he was speaking into a void, a chasm that absorbed every syllable before it could reach her.

Ava...

She couldn't hear him.

And he couldn't hear her.

It was then that his exhaustion finally won out, and he slipped into a deep slumber with only one thought.

Consequences...

14

THE PAYMENT

One Year Later...

Surrounded by sheer nothingness, by utter freedom, Asher basked in the sun, his eyes closed. It seemed there was only empty space between him and that great light, as if he might reach up and actually touch its heavenly aura.

But the mysteries beyond the world were not meant for him. The ranger was firmly tethered to Verda.

And a dragon.

Avandriell tucked in her wings, dipped her horned head, and corkscrewed into a vertical dive. The clouds burst apart and it seemed all of Verda was there to greet them, arms open. A carpet of green blanketed the land, stretching in every direction in its reach for dominance.

The Evermoore.

Home to man and beast alike, the forest lay at Illian's heart. It was also home to many memories, good and bad as far as Asher was concerned. Today, however, was to be the making of another good memory. It had been some years since the ranger had looked forward to the payment he had earned, and this one had been twelve months in the making.

Allowing Asher to catch his breath, Avandriell fanned her wings and settled into a comfortable glide, the membranes between her bones flapping rapidly in the high wind. About a mile ahead and straight down was the crown jewel of The Evermoore, the gem within the heart: Lirian.

With no natural defences barring the forest itself, the city was accessible from all sides, offering only two roads in the west and the south. Sprawled at the base of a small mountain, its buildings and towers were a combination of light grey stone and wood, its many chimneys at work funnelling plenty of smoke.

Of all the cities in the world, Lirian might have been the closest thing to a home in Asher's opinion. Not that the ranger wanted a home. The realm was too vast and full of wonders to make roots in any one place and, in truth, he felt Avandriell was his home. Their place was in the sky, where they could soar together for all time.

The ranger patted her scales. While it was a comfort to share in her feelings and get a sense of her emotions, he missed the sound of her voice terribly. A year on and the void between them was still too far. A year on and he was still kept awake with fear that they would never bridge it, that her voice was lost to him forever.

Feeling his apprehension, Avandriell turned her head to lay a single eye on him. She could but growl or roar, unable to articulate her thoughts. Asher was warmed, however, by the notes of hope that crossed what remained of their bond. Better that, he thought, than the anger she could send his way, as she had done often since defeating the Leviathan.

Lirian was so close now as to discern people in the streets.

Asher envisioned his companion's intentions, glimpsing the image in his mind. "The streets are too narrow," he warned her, calling over the wind. "You can't walk through them."

The dragon glanced back at him again, a snort escaping her nostrils. *Of course I can*, he imagined her to respond.

"You'll destroy people's homes just trying to turn a corner!"

The dragon grunted and banked to take them into a sharper descent.

"Avandriell?" he said questioningly. Damned if the void between them wasn't as infuriating as it was upsetting. "I know what you're thinking!" he yelled. "It isn't fitting for a dragon to sit idly by the road and wait for her companion like some horse tied to a tree!"

A single and affirmative growl rippled out from her chest.

Asher sighed. "There's a spot at the western end of Ruskin Street," the ranger explained. "It branches north and south. If you land *slowly*," he emphasised, "you should be able to touch down without destroying anything. It's a straight walk from there."

As she would upon arriving anywhere, the dragon swept once around the city, her speed disturbing the tops of the great pines. It gave the people enough time to spread the word and create something of a frenzy. Asher still didn't enjoy it, his old instincts always urging him to pass through the world unnoticed.

It was more than that when it came to Lirian.

While Avandriell could only see it in his memories, Asher recalled his assault on the city with terrible vividness. He could still feel the heat of Malliath's fire as the black dragon brought wrath and ruin down on the good people of Lirian. It would have been fair, he thought, if there remained some level of trepidation when it came to dragons.

Yet that was not the case.

From north to south, all of Illian knew the role dragons like Avandriell had played in The Fated War. Athis had become a popular name in times since his sacrifice, and many a tavern had changed their name to The Red Dragon, his likeness painted upon their signs.

And so the people of Lirian cheered as Avandriell set down in their midst, her presence sending a shudder through the city's foundations. And their arrival wasn't without a touch of destruction, as Asher had feared. The dragon's tail ploughed through an empty stall, reducing it to splinters, while the tips of her wings dislodged numerous bricks in a chimney and scratched a handful of slates on a roof.

Asher winced all the more when his companion tucked in her wings and pulled free someone's gutter system. "This is why I said—"

Avandriell cut him off with a look, her neck twisted to lay both of her golden eyes on him.

"I know, I know," he said, extrapolating from her emotions alone. "This day will stay with them for the rest of their lives…"

Asher still made a mental note to pay the owners a visit before they left and provide the coin for repairs.

Not even halfway down Ruskin Street, it became clear to the ranger that there was royalty present in the city. Archers had taken up stations on several rooftops, their position giving them a vantage of the streets either side as well as Ruskin. Every alleyway had been blocked by a cart and a pair of soldiers bearing the sigil of the flaming sword. Patrols of threes and fours walked up and down, always scrutinising the passers by.

Their number was most concentrated around one building in particular. Single storey and detached from those either side, its woodwork possessed a solid look about it, the timbers of its porch thick and newly fashioned. A carpenter had also seen to the steps, replacing the broken panels. From his saddle, Asher could easily see that the roof was obviously brand new, its every shingle replaced and the chimney re-pointed.

As the soldiers were bowing in Avandriell's presence, Asher climbed down and set his feet to Lirian's rich earth. Muddy across the rim, his customary green cloak fell into place behind his heels while the arrows in his quiver were jostled by the short jump.

Standing at the foot of the steps, Asher was confronted by yet more memories, and glad of them he was.

The door, freshly painted, was the exact shade of green Russell Maybury had always employed. He could see him standing there from a time long past, a welcoming smile on his face and the offer of a bed for the night.

Craning his neck, the ranger had a smile of his own as he looked upon the tavern's sign.

The Pick-Axe.

A local artist had clearly been paid to produce a new one, the old sign having been left to the elements for too many years. Much like the rest of it had been.

"Do not hold to your regrets," came a familiar voice, turning the ranger to his left, where Galanör Reveeri approached him on light feet.

"Have I become so easy to read?" Asher replied.

"Only to those who know you," the elf replied with a warm smile. "You have not neglected this place," he went on. "It needed time to rest in Russell's absence. Not so it might forget him, but so it might get a feel for the world left in his wake, left in his deeds." Galanör looked from the Pick-Axe to the ranger. "It is in *your* deeds that Russell Maybury is still remembered. Not bricks and mortar."

"This would have made him happy though," Asher added, his smile yet to fade.

The green door opened and a familiar figure stepped out onto the porch. "It's just as I remember it!" the King of Illian declared proudly.

"And I," Asher replied, ascending to the porch while Galanör bowed in Avandriell's presence.

"I would also have paid you *double* what this has cost for slaying the Leviathan," Vighon added, before the two men met in a tight embrace.

"This is reward enough," the ranger told him, keen to look inside.

The northman was right: it was just as it had been. Fully stocked, the bar stretched across the adjacent wall as he walked in, a welcoming sight to any and all who wandered the world. The tavern expanded both left and right of the bar, offering booths, tables and even a spot for merry bands to play their music and bards to tell their tales.

In the far left corner there still sat a door, as there always had been. Asher knew it opened to a stairwell that descended into the Pick-Axe's cellar and a collection of rooms that had long catered to the needs of rangers.

"It's all down there," Inara informed him, rising from one of the tables.

Asher happily greeted the queen with a hug, accepting a graceful kiss on his cheek. She gripped his hands a moment longer, until

Adilandra crashed into his hip. Athis soon followed, the two clashing together hand-in-hand in a brief contest of strength. The young man was certainly getting stronger, but it wasn't his day to beat the ranger.

Falling into laughter and embraces, Asher was overwhelmed by his surroundings and, as always, the love he felt from his friends.

The latter would never cease to surprise him.

Aenwyn was a welcome sight as she broke through the young Draqaros and greeted the ranger as a warrior would, their forearms gripped in each other's hands. Slaying a creature so foul and wicked as a Leviathan together was no small thing. Asher felt their bond had grown and he welcomed it, respecting the elf as much as he did Galanör.

They talked him through the refurbishments, including the new kitchen they had installed behind the bar. He was then taken on a tour of the cellar, where the rooms had been furnished to accept temporary residents—rangers all he was assured. They had spared no expense remodelling the small bar area, where rangers could get together without the hustle and bustle of the busy tavern above.

At the back of the cellar, round the corner, Asher looked upon the armoury. Russell had tended to it for years, amassing weapons, armour, and all manner of supplies for the realm's monster hunters. Just as it had been, its walls were, again, lined with everything one might need to hunt, fight, and survive all manner of beast.

To his astonishment, he discovered the alcove on his left was similarly stocked, only it had been filled with identical green cloaks, brown boots and leather armour. Three quivers hung from hooks, all brimming with arrows, and there stood a cabinet displaying a variety of knives, small axes, and different types of rope.

His locker.

It had been the only thing he asked of Russell when he handed over the tavern's management to him. Diligently, Russell had done just that, allowing the ranger to find shelter, warm food, good company, and fresh equipment to replace whatever he had lost or broken on the last hunt.

Returned to The Pick-Axe's main floor, Asher took it all in again, feeling that he had stepped into memory. Had he ever received a better reward for killing a monster?

"I can still remember the fight I got into right here," Vighon said, standing just off from the bar. "Alijah had cheated his way through a game of Galant and been caught." The king chuckled to himself. "There was no fighting your way out of Russell's grip once he had you." The northman then pointed at one of the booths. "I met you for the first time right there," he said, turning to look at Galanör.

"Did we?" the elf questioned, a mischievous grin on his face. "I recall meeting a scruffy young man who had no idea what he was getting himself into."

"You're not wrong," the king replied humbly.

Asher found himself at the bar, his hands laid out on the smooth wood. He was staring at the blank spot between the bottles and tankards. The hooks were still there, screwed into the wall, but the pick-axe itself was missing.

"Asher?" Inara called softly.

The ranger gestured at the empty space. "I meant to return from Dhenaheim with the pick-axe," he explained. "It was years before we actually left though. Avandriell grew so much while we were there. Both of us were eager to see anything other than snow by the end. Damned if I didn't drink too much dwarven mead," he added with some levity.

Inara was smiling at him, and knowingly so.

"What?"

The queen looked pointedly at the bottles behind the bar. It was subtle at first, but the vibrations soon grew, rattling the glass. Then came the sound of horns. They were followed by drums and the distant chorus of trumpets.

Asher was familiar with that particular cacophony.

"You didn't?" he asked, locking eyes with Inara.

It was Vighon who replied, making his way to the green door. "He would have been furious if he discovered we re-opened The Pick-Axe without him."

Asher could feel Avandriell's emotional response to whatever she was seeing outside. Happiness. Pure and simple happiness.

Their years freeing the halls of Dhenaheim from its many monsters had endeared the dragon to the ways of the dwarf. The two were akin in many ways—more ways than Asher cared to admit about his companion.

Sunlight flooded Ruskin Street, along with many of its inhabitants, who clambered to see the marching column of dwarves. Asher watched from the end of the porch, his old eyes finding an old friend.

Leading his people through the streets of Lirian, Doran Heavybelly sat astride his long-favoured mount, Pig. His crown of silvyr shone under the sun, a contrast to his armour of dull black leather, with only a few, modest, accents of gold here and there. Strapped to the back of his saddle was Andaljor, the weapon of his ancestors.

All at once, the marching band and procession of hundreds came to a stop. A single dwarf stepped out of line, his head held high, though his mouth could not be seen for the bushy beard he sported.

"King Doran Heavybelly, son o' Dorain! Orc-slayer! Master o' the northern snows an' commander o' the dwarven legions—"

"A'right, a'right," Doran interrupted, his gloved hand patting the air. "Shut it. They know who I am."

The dwarven king dismounted and, without even looking to those on the porch—two of whom reigned over the very soil he was standing on—genuflected before Avandriell. As one, the few hundred dwarves behind him did the same and bent the knee, fists clenched against chests.

"Should any dwarf call Dhenaheim their home," Doran announced, "they are forever indebted to ye, Avandriell, daughter o' Garganafan. Without yer tooth an' claw, our lands would still be in the grips o' fiends."

Asher cleared his throat.

Doran glanced at the ranger, though his one eye did not stray from Avandriell for long. "Still kickin' around with this one, eh? Don' let 'im hold ye back."

The dragon issued a guttural chocking noise that reverberated up and down her throat, displaying her amusement.

"Good King Vighon!" The son of Dorain went on to greet. "The even better Queen Inara! I thank ye on behalf o' all me folk for the invitation to this grand openin'!"

The king of Dhenaheim climbed The Pick-Axe's steps and accepted their greetings in return, including their compliments regarding his elaborate escort and the manner of his arrival. It was only proper that he embrace them first, and with so many watching, but the dwarf was soon laughing as he clasped Asher's hand and dragged the ranger into a crushing embrace.

"It's not enough that ye be crowned a hero from Silvyr Hall to Syla's Gate!" he complained, looking up at Asher. "Ye've got to go an' be the slayer o' Leviathans too!"

Asher wasn't one for shouldering compliments, regardless of how they were delivered. "I wasn't fighting alone," he said, eyeing Galanör, Aenwyn and, of course, Avandriell, who watched from the street.

"An' ye never will," Doran replied, a warm and reassuring tone in his gravelly voice. His eye widened when a girl of his height pushed through the group. "Come 'ere, ye rascal!" he growled giddily. Princess Adilandra was quickly buried within the dwarf's bear-like hug. "Right! Let's be seein' the place! I've travelled six hundred miles for this—ye can bet I'm thirsty!"

Doran's presence only amplified the history of the place, bringing The Pick-Axe to life in a way no other could. His very voice seemed to soak into the wooden frames and beams, reminding the tavern of what it could be. Like Asher, he was given a tour of the place, to which he gave every aspect his seal of approval. Also like Asher, the dwarf eventually found himself standing before that empty space above the bar.

"Are you running this place or am I?" Asher jested, daring not to tread any further into the past, where he and Doran had been forced to kill their old friend and free him of the lycan curse.

The dwarven king cracked a laugh and turned to the green door. "Bori! Orlin! Dili!"

Asher narrowed his eyes, waiting for the three named dwarves to enter the tavern. They did so at the same time. It created something of a spacing issue, with all three of them vying for enough room to permit them entry. They jostled and argued, their broad shoulders and large heads colliding and shoving each other.

"For the love o' Grarfath!" Doran complained.

One after the other, the trio of dwarves fell through the doorway and presented themselves to the many royal figures. Asher had to blink, sure that he was seeing three of the same dwarf. They each sported long hair and beards down to their belt buckles, all of the same rich copper, just as they shared the same blue eyes and freckled face.

"This is Bori, Orlin, and Dili," Doran introduced, gesturing to each one as he named them.

In response, the dwarves repeated their names, except they were not standing in the order the king had believed them to be.

Asher maintained his look of expectation as the tavern fell quiet.

Doran turned to the Draqaros. "Ye didn' tell 'im?"

"We thought it best you explain," Inara answered.

The dwarven king shrugged and returned his attention to Asher. "Ye own the place, aye? But ye'll never find anyone who can run it the way Rus did. He were stronger than any man an' he had sharp eyes to boot—he missed nothin'." Doran side-stepped and swept his hands across the brothers. "They've the strength to keep order an' between the three o' 'em they're not likely to miss anything."

Asher shifted his focus to the three dwarves. "You *want* to run The Pick-Axe?"

"Oh aye!"

"O' course!"

The smaller of the three simply nodded.

"Dili don' talk," Doran said bluntly. "Considerin' there's three o' 'em ye'll come to count that as a blessin'," he added out of the side of his mouth.

"The Pick-Axe is legendary," Bori stated.

"Many o' the king's tales begin right 'ere in this very room," Orlin commented.

"They come from a long line o' brewers," Doran told the ranger. "They even had their own tavern in Grimwhal before the war. They're good dwarves, Asher. Ye can trust 'em to run the place right. How Rus would 'ave wanted."

It dawned on Asher then that it was officially up to him, the owner. He stood a little straighter, doing his best to take the moment seriously. They were filling very big boots.

"I'll offer you the same deal I offered Russell Maybury. The tavern is yours. The profits are yours. The *losses* are yours. The cellar belongs to rangers and the armoury remains stocked."

"Deal!" Bori and Orlin said as one, with Dili hammering fist into hand, a beaming smile beneath his thick beard.

Doran clapped his hands together. "Excellent! Oh, wait! Dili, fetch the…" The king was nodding at the front door.

Dili hurried off, letting the daylight spill into the tavern for a minute.

"Ye forgot somethin'," Doran said to the ranger. "I've been keepin' it for jus' such a moment as this."

Upon Dili's return, the dwarf now held an object horizontally in both hands. A pick-axe. It was old by the rust on the iron head and the wooden haft was chipped and scored by numerous tallies. Every line was a monster slain.

Doran let Dili present it to Asher. "Ye can't 'ave The Pick-Axe, without *the* pick-axe. Put it where it belongs, laddy."

Asher took in hand Russell's weapon of choice. It was heavier than he remembered. It was also whole, the haft having been repaired by dwarven craftsmen. Gladly, the ranger walked behind the bar and placed it on its mantle.

"An' jus' like that," Doran declared, "Russell's home! Let's get to openin' the joint! Drinks!"

Asher beamed. "Drinks," he agreed.

The merriment that ensued was raucous, as it would be with a few hundred thirsty dwarves. The Pick-Axe was soon filled, crammed from wall to wall with Lirians and dwarves alike, keeping Bori, Orlin, and Dili on their toes. More than anyone, they three looked the happiest, despite being swamped by customers and demands.

Before the celebration could begin in earnest, Asher made sure a cup was raised between him, Galanör, and Aenwyn. "To Hadarax of the Oden seed," he cheered as they kicked their tankards together. "May he find rest in what I can only imagine are the largest halls in the afterlife."

"To Hadarax," the elves said in unison.

Asher spared the Giant his thoughts for a moment, holding off that first sip. His sacrifice had not only saved Avandriell but also shown him the only way to beat the beast. He hoped to one day meet more from the Gondolian Horde.

For all the great moments that occurred over the next few hours, there was none that solidified The Pick-Axe's return more than the presence of one particular individual.

Pig.

Doran's mount snuffled at the ground, following his nose until he found discarded tankards and bottles that he could tip into his slobbery mouth. The Warhog seemed entirely oblivious to the other patrons, his girth knocking many aside as he navigated the heady scents of ale and mead from one side of the tavern to the other. He was chased out more than once by Orlin, who was unaware that Dili continued to affectionately coax the Warhog back inside.

As would often happen at crowded events, Asher found himself in conversation with Inara alone, the two enjoying a booth of their own. She smiled fondly at Vighon, who looked very much at home amidst the rowdy dwarves, his son shoulder to shoulder and with a drink in hand.

"How goes plans with Erador?" the ranger asked.

"The new harbours are already underway, though construction in the west is swifter than our own. They already have three cities on the coast, so their docks simply require expansion. We have begun gathering materials and labour just south of Snowfell, but the town itself is in need of as much investment as the docks themselves. Things are looking better in the south," she added hopefully. "Ameeraska is set to be the jewel of The Arid Lands thanks to its access to The Hox."

Asher sipped his drink, thinking of how different Snowfell—a small and sleepy town—would look drastically different in a few years time. And trade in the south would always be a good thing, allowing their culture to be appreciated by all while gaining some prosperity at the same time.

"The dwarves are not to be left out, of course," Inara continued. "They're building their own harbour south of The Whispering Mountains."

Asher put his tankard down. "Dwarves. Sailing?"

The queen laughed quietly to herself. "I can't imagine it either, but they want the trade..."

The ranger nodded along, already amused at the thought of dwarves trying to make sense of the sea.

Inara was looking at him intently, her expression having grown serious. "It's been a year now," she said. "Can you hear each other yet?"

Asher was slow to respond. "No."

Inara looked genuinely saddened. "What about your magic? Has it returned at all?"

The ranger glanced at his fingers, gripped to the tankard. Every day he had tried to create something as meagre as a spark and every day he had failed.

"I can't feel it anymore," he finally answered. "It used to be just *there*. Now it's a void."

"But you can still feel Avandriell?"

"Deeply," the ranger was pleased to report. "We just can't speak to each other. It's... infuriating. It's also been very isolating for Avandriell. She can't speak to anyone through me."

"It *will* return," Inara said confidently.

"You don't know that," Asher pointed out, shying away from any thread of hope.

"It returned for my grandmother," Inara countered.

"Adilandra was a thousand years old and an elf. While my age is very much up for debate, I'm certainly no elf."

"You're a *Dragon Rider.*"

Asher shot her a pointed look.

"In all but name," the queen was quick to add. "It *will* return." Inara tilted her head, scrutinising him. "You truly doubt it?"

"I can't see in the dark anymore," he stated evenly.

Inara sat back, her mind clearly assessing the situation from another angle. "But you've always had the Nightseye elixir in your bones. Even when The Crow resurrected you it was *still* in your bones."

"It's been *spent,*" the ranger said, hoping his choice of words would convey the severity of his situation. "I expelled every ounce of magic I had and then some. It's as if my bones have… dried up. I can't use magic and I'm just as blind as everyone else now."

Inara sat in thought for a moment longer. "Avandriell remains a being of magic," she eventually explained. "Even if your end of the bond is frayed, her end will be building that bridge for the both of you. It just needs *time.* I'm sure of it. And," she added, her tone lightening, "losing the Nightseye elixir means you've cut that last cord between you and Nightfall. I see that as a good thing."

Asher wasn't entirely sure he agreed with the latter.

Inara's hand landed atop his own. "I'm sorry it came to this. If we had known the cost to you both we would never have asked you to slay the Leviathan."

"I knew the consequences," the ranger replied glumly. "Besides, the world just got a lot bigger. And a lot finer," he said, raising his tankard to The Pick-Axe itself.

"If you had asked, we would have seen to this regardless of the Leviathan," Inara replied.

"I know."

Asher smiled and not just because he glimpsed Adilandra astride Pig. It was quite something to be among friends—to be loved.

"Come on," Doran drawled, his voice drowning out all others. "It's to be a story o' the ages! Let's be hearin' it from one whose blade tasted the fiend's foul blood!"

The dwarven king was cajoling a somewhat reluctant-looking Galanör towards the small stage where many a ranger had told their tale in exchange for a night in the cellar.

"Gather round!" the son of Dorain yelled. "We're to hear the slayin' o' the last Leviathan!"

Invited by the open arm of her husband, Inara moved to depart their booth, though she squeezed the ranger's hand before leaving. "It *will* return," she repeated.

Joined by Aenwyn, who brought him a fresh drink, Asher listened to Galanör's accounting of their time in Erador and the battle with the beast. He was glad to hear the elf speak highly of Hadarax and detail his saving of Avandriell and, therefore, the rest of them. The tale was met with more merriment and no end of songs from the dwarven contingent.

Thusly, The Pick-Axe's grand re-opening continued for three more days. Asher enjoyed his stay beneath the tavern while the royal family temporarily retreated to rooms arranged for them by the lord of Lirian. But day and evening were spent together, a joyous time well-earned.

Given the distance they had covered, Doran came to an agreement with Vighon and Inara that the dwarves would remain in Lirian for a few weeks more, camping just beyond its borders. The rulers of Illian, however, were needed back at the capital, where there was still so much to do in preparation for the impending trade routes and alliance with Erador.

Deciding they would see them off in a deserving fashion, Asher and Avandriell took to the skies and escorted the Draqaros through and beyond The Evermoore's boundary. Their party was almost as large as Doran's, easily tracked from on high until they began to fade along their northern path.

Avandriell banked back to the south and began the return journey to Lirian, where they might spend some more time with Doran and his kin. It had been the best of days, their company of such quality to have nourished the soul.

Asher drank it all in, along with a view so few had ever seen. So marvellous was the face of Illian that the ranger almost missed it.

A whisper.

A trick of the wind?

His imagination?

He looked about the land that stretched beneath them, as if he might locate the source of the small voice. It came again, reminding him of the first time he entered the egg chamber in Drakanan.

The whisper grew, though the words remained muffled. It was a tune, he knew. Humming, perhaps.

Unbridled was the smile that pulled at Asher's cheeks, his revelation a rising sun on a dreary vista. It was a familiar tune, a song of the dwarves that had blasted out of The Pick-Axe for three days.

Avandriell was singing...

PHILIP C. QUAINTRELL

*Hear more from Philip C. Quaintrell including
book releases and exclusive content:*

◇◇◇◇◇◇◇◇◇◇◇◇◇◇◇◇

PHILIPCQUAINTRELL.COM

ABOUT THE AUTHOR

Philip C. Quaintrell is the author of the epic fantasy series, The Echoes Saga, as well as the Terran Cycle sci-fi series. He was born in Cheshire in 1989 and started his career as an emergency nurse.

Having always been a fan of fantasy and sci-fi fiction, Philip started to find himself feeling frustrated as he read books, wanting to delve into the writing himself to tweak characters and storylines. He decided to write his first novel as a hobby to escape from nursing and found himself swept away into the world he'd created. Even now, he talks about how the characters tell him what they're going to do next, rather than the other way around.

With his first book written, and a good few rejected agency submissions under his belt, he decided to throw himself in at the deep end and self-publish. 2 months and £60 worth of sales in, he took his wife out to dinner to celebrate an achievement ticked off his bucket list - blissfully unaware this was just the beginning.

Fast forward 12 months and he was self-publishing book 1 of his fantasy series (The Echoes Saga; written purely as a means to combat his sci-fi writers' block). With no discernible marketing except the 'Amazon algorithm', the book was in the amazon bestsellers list in at least 4 countries within a month. The Echoes Saga has now surpassed 700k copies sold worldwide, has an option agreement for a potential TV-series in the pipeline and Amazon now puts Philip's sales figures in the top 1.8% of self-published authors worldwide.

Philip lives in Cheshire, England with his wife and two children. He still finds time between naps and wiping snot off his clothes to remain a movie aficionado and comic book connoisseur, and is hoping this is still just the beginning.

AUTHOR NOTES

This is truly for those who have read The Echoes Saga and simply needed more. I enjoyed writing every sentence of this and it was a real joy to spend 46,000 words on just Asher and Avandriell. Getting one book of them in the saga just wasn't enough.

I see this as the first novella in a series of novellas that I imagine will act as stepping stones that will bridge the gap between The Echoes Saga and the next big series I write—obviously a post Echoes story.

Things might change of course—I'm always at the mercy of my imagination.

Either way, this novella is not the last you've seen of Asher and Avandriell!

I hope you enjoyed the story as much as you did getting to see this new part of the timeline. Tackling the last Leviathan felt like something the future of Verda just needed. Of course, you can't kill something as ancient and powerful as a demon of the deep world without consequences. You'll have to wait until future instalments/ sagas to see how things evolve for Asher from here on.

Can he use magic? Will he ever see in the dark again?

The future remains unwritten—literally. While you wait for that, I would greatly appreciate any reviews you might leave on Amazon et al. I am still choosing to follow the path of the indie author which is allowing me to write full time, and your reviews help to fuel that. In return, I promise a never-ending stream of quality stories.

Also, if you would like a shiny copy of this book, it is being exclusively sold through The Broken Binding in hardback and every one will be signed by yours truly.

Now, if you'll excuse me, I have to get back to writing A Time of Dragons: Book 3!

Until the next time...

VERDA TIMELINE

A TIME OF DRAGONS

12,000 YEARS

THE RANGER ARCHIVES

12 DAYS

THE ECHOES SAGA

  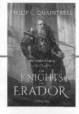  

NOVELLA STORIES

3 YEARS

Made in United States
Orlando, FL
15 April 2025

60555754R00097